Praise for

# PALACE OF FLIES

"*Palace of Flies* is one of those rare biographical novels that bring a whole world to life in a way that lingers in memory. This is an important book in which Walter Kappacher holds a peculiarly sharp mirror to the past and shows us, as all good historical novels do, an eerily astute glimpse at our present."

—JAY PARINI,
author of *Borges and Me*

"Walter Kappacher's novel triumphs in portraying a middle-aged writer who balances the most intimate behavior—insomnia, indigestion—with the grandest of artistic ambitions. He achieves a special pathos by deliberately not underlining what we know—that the fifty-year-old protagonist is a few years from a tragic death and that everything he represents will be burned alive. Kappacher captures a now almost unimaginable sensibility with absolute coherence one hundred years later."

—ANTHONY HEILBUT,
author of *Thomas Mann: Eros and Literature* and
*Exiled in Paradise*

"Kappacher's sensitive channeling of Hugo von Hofmannsthal's voice and sensibility illuminates the difficulties of a creative mind to come to terms with a radically changing world.

Michael P. Steinberg's brilliantly concise introduction anchors the kaleidoscopic glimmer of the author's memories in the turmoil of the first quarter of the twentieth century."

—GITTA HONEGGER,
author of *Thomas Bernhard: The Making of an Austrian*
and translator of Nobel laureate Elfriede Jelinek

"In this elaborate, intellectual portrait of the collapsed Austro-Hungarian empire, Hugo von Hofmannsthal emerges as a man whose accomplishments and eloquence have left him utterly unprepared for the desolation of history. A meditation on the artist's struggle to bring to life one's own age, even as that age dissolves, and to make use of time as time makes use of us. A beautiful book."

—ADAM KLEIN,
author of *The Medicine Burns* and *Tiny Ladies*

"A masterpiece of contemporary story-telling."

—*DER STANDARD*

"You don't have to be a Hofmannsthal connoisseur or even a lover to fall under the spell."

—*ORF* AUSTRIAN RADIO

"Walter Kappacher . . . is the most serious author I know. And at the same time there's the paradox that it's a seriousness that's lightly worn."

—PETER HANDKE,
winner of the Nobel Prize for Literature

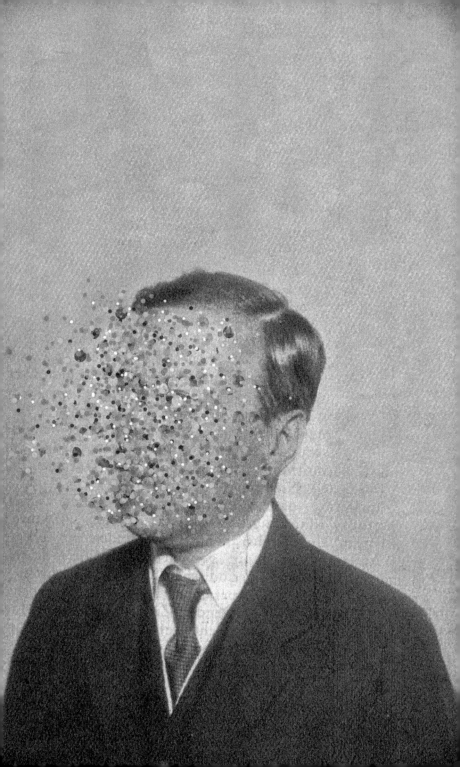

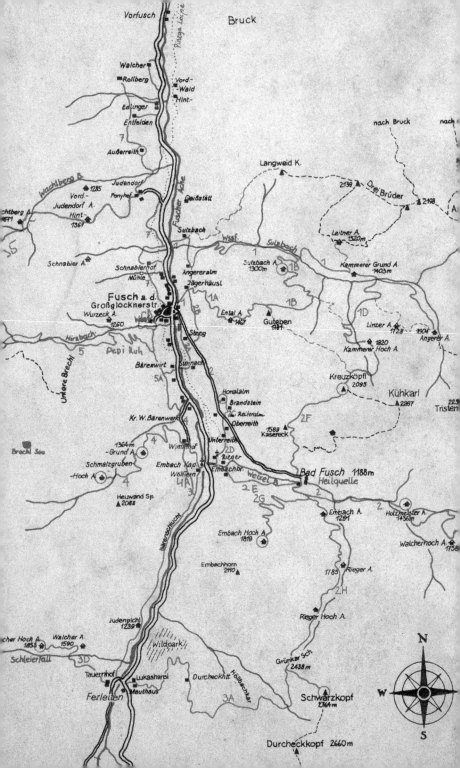

# PALACE OF FLIES

A NOVEL

## WALTER KAPPACHER

INTRODUCTION BY
MICHAEL P. STEINBERG

TRANSLATED FROM THE GERMAN BY
GEORG BAUER

NEW VESSEL PRESS
NEW YORK

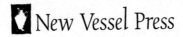

New Vessel Press

www.newvesselpress.com

First published in German as *Der Fliegenpalast*
Copyright © 2009 Residenz Verlag GmbH Salzburg—Wien
Translation copyright © 2022 Georg Bauer
Introduction copyright © 2022 Michael P. Steinberg
Published with the support of the Austrian Cultural Forum New York

austrian cultural forum™

Library of Congress Cataloging-in-Publication Data
Kappacher, Walter
[Der Fliegenpalast, English]
Palace of Flies/Walter Kappacher; introduction by Michael P. Steinberg; translation by Georg Bauer.
p. cm.
ISBN 978-1-954404-02-1

Library of Congress Control Number 2021941850
1. Austria—Fiction

Map © Gemeinde Fusch an der Grossglocknerstrasse

# INTRODUCTION

## MICHAEL P. STEINBERG

Echoes have unpredictable relations to time. When the sound of our own voice returns to us, we hear it as the voice of a stranger. The return of a childhood memory, on the other hand, may seem immediate, even when the passage of time is multiplied by seismic cultural shifts, the disappearance of an epoch and its way of life.

The final crash of Austria's empire and persistent old Habsburg regime in 1918 is perhaps the strongest modern example of such a seismic disruption. The writer Hugo von Hofmannsthal remains possibly its most paradigmatic voice: its analyst as well as its symptom. As a teenager and a leading prodigy of his generation, Hofmannsthal was the archetypal spirit of the Viennese fin de siècle, a matinée idol among the literati of the imperial capital in the 1890s. Both a product and diagnostician of widespread cultural malaise, he produced apocalyptic writings that chronologically preceded the actual political apocalypse and the onset of the small Austrian "republic that no one wanted."

Set in this postapocalyptic world, Walter Kappacher's *Palace of Flies* finds Hofmannsthal returning in 1924, at age fifty, to a resort near Salzburg where he had spent summers of his youth with his parents. Here, time and otherness, intimacy and alienation echo loudly, just as they have as prime ingredients of the twentieth century literary imagination.

Six years after the end of the First World War and the empire's collapse, the melancholy poet, playwright, and librettist cannot bring himself to write. He naps between dizzy spells and enjoys only the company of a young physician who has recently returned to Austria after a formative period in the still-new world, namely the United States.

Conversing, the writer and the doctor repeatedly invoke the former's little remembered novella of 1907, *Letters of the Man Who Returned* [*Briefe des Zurückgekehrten*], an account (of similar length to Kappacher's own story) of a businessman who returns to Europe following a long professional period abroad, finding himself especially alienated by Germany and consoled only by color (this itself an allusion to Johann Wolfgang von Goethe's color theory, or *Farbenlehre*) and in particular by the strong colors of several paintings of Vincent van Gogh. Much better known and remembered is that story's twin: Hofmannsthal's 1901 "Letter of Lord Chandos," an epistolary treatise addressed to Sir Francis Bacon bemoaning a crisis of language and the resulting uselessness of the written word: a performative contradiction if there ever was one and a modernist cri de coeur in baroque costume.

Between these two mannered works came the play *Elektra*, after Sophocles, in which the prodigious and still precious poet was transfigured, in the poet Michael

Hamburger's phrase, into a "barbarous visionary," exclaiming, through some of the greatest dramatic poetry in the German language, the impossibility of reconstituting political and familial order following the self-cannibalization of the old regime. Refusing to disavow the cry of Lord Chandos about the senescence of the word, Hofmannsthal offered his play to the composer Richard Strauss, with whom he would go on to collaborate on a series of operas and who under-girded *Elektra*'s text with music of truly terrible beauty.

Hofmannsthal's and Strauss's creative will, and indeed their sense of comedy and wit, did in fact survive the end of empire more than most later scholarship—and perhaps more than Walter Kappacher—allows. But they were overtaken by another project, a different plan for the rescue of German culture following what Karl Kraus famously dubbed "the last days of mankind." This was the Salzburg Festival, the annual month-long season of opera, theater, and concerts aimed at constructing a new cultural identity for a vastly shrunken Austria. Hofmannsthal was the principal spiritual and institutional founder. The festival was inaugurated in 1920 with *Jedermann*, Hofmannsthal's creaky 1911 version of the English morality play *Everyman*, staged by Max Reinhardt on the steps of the Cathedral of Salzburg (with the permission of the bishop), to the lasting glory of sentimental conservatism and with the immediate and occasionally recurring antisemitic invective. (Hofmannsthal's great-grandfather Isaak Löw Hofmann was an ennobled textile merchant whose son converted to Catholicism and married into the lower Milanese nobility; Reinhardt, né Goldmann, was the Baden-born son of a Hungarian Jewish merchant, Strauss the son of a musician and a brewer's daughter from Munich for whom all sacred culture was uncannily irrelevant.)

Echoes often come with ghosts, and there are many throughout *Palace of Flies*—both Hofmannsthal's ghosts as well as Kappacher's. Jewish ancestry remained one of Hofmannsthal's ghosts, alongside the full German literary tradition with the figure of Goethe at its summit. So did what he called "the Austrian ideal," rendered in stone by the baroque architecture of Salzburg and its Italianate sensuality. According to this view, Germany, or more precisely Prussia, started World War I and its ultimate debacle; Austria and its spirit, even if decapitated from its lands, would survive and perform from the stages of Salzburg, with the city itself reconsecrated as The Great Theater of the World: *Das grosse Salzburger Welttheater*.

By 1927 Hofmannsthal would politicize his agenda as a program of "conservative revolution," egged on by the post-1923 economic crisis of Germany and Austria (the cause, among more serious consequences, of the cancellation of the 1924 festival in Salzburg, as Kappacher's story recounts), and the encouragement of figures, also mentioned in *Palace of Flies*, such as the literary cult figure Stefan George and the crackpot Rudolf Pannwitz. George supplied the National Socialists with much of their language, including *Das neue Reich*, the title of his 1928 book of poems. Yet he disdained the movement itself as a philistine enactment of his lofty ideals, paralleling the views of two of his acolytes, the Stauffenberg brothers. George's name survives today mostly among eye-rolling literary historians. Rudolf Pannwitz is justifiably forgotten. (I did myself find, in a Salzburg bookstore in the 1980s, an attractive in-print edition of Pannwitz's *Crisis of European Culture*, which, perversely, I bought.)

Rudolf Borchardt—with whom Hofmannsthal quarreled in 1924, thereby producing a component of the melancholy of Kappacher's protagonist—is a more serious and more abiding, if less well-known, figure. Aesthete son of a hostile Jewish father, he became an acolyte of the slightly older Hugo von Hofmannsthal and arrived for a visit in 1901, the year of Lord Chandos. He lived the post–World War I years in Tuscany, admired the fascist regime, and in 1933 presented Mussolini with his own translation of Dante's *Divine Comedy*, an ingratiating gesture that did not save him from deportation in 1944.

The current, modest Borchardt renaissance is eclipsed, however, by the surge of interest in Harry Graf Kessler, the publisher, diplomat, bon vivant, chronicler, and diarist par excellence of fin-de-siècle and interwar Berlin. Carl Burckhardt, scion of the patrician Basel family and a significantly more sober figure invoked often in the novella, had encountered Hofmannsthal as a young diplomat posted in Vienna after 1918. His later career proved as controversial as it was distinguished. Serving, alternately, as High Commissioner of the Free City of Danzig in the late 1930s and then as President of the International Committee of the

Red Cross during the Second World War and thereafter, he resisted any condemnation of Nazism or the Third Reich as their crimes became evident. "A diplomat and known careerist," Samuel Moyn has recently written, "Burckhardt harbored a traditional anti-Semitism and such hatred of communism that he regarded German Nazism as a bulwark of civilization and a necessary evil."

Walter Kappacher's own most prominent ghost is Hofmannsthal's most eminent analyst: the Austrian philosopher-novelist Hermann Broch. Commissioned in his American exile to write an essay on his aristocratic forebear, Broch confessed that repulsion had given way to some attraction in the way that "a lesbian liaison develops between a lady and her chambermaid." The result is the cornerstone study *Hofmannsthal und seine Zeit* [ . . . and his Time], in which the writer figures as both spokesperson and symptom of his time, of the passage from late nineteenth-century historicism to fin-de-siècle modernism to postimperial conservatism, from the emergence of a child prodigy to the fate of "a bad poet."

Broch reserved especially acerbic words for Hofmannsthal's *Jedermann* and its annual performances in front of the cathedral (a practice that persists to the current day), describing it as a costume play not so much for the stage itself as for the audience, who collectively continue to perform their own conservative revolution by dressing for the occasion in the folkloric *trachten*. In 2000, the Salzburg Festival's maverick artistic director Gérard Mortier made the same complaint, describing the *Jedermann* audiences as sui generis incarnations of the Austrian political right who remythologize themselves through the ritual of their annual attendance.

Broch's pathbreaking work proved seminal to Carl E. Schorske's now classic *Fin-de-siècle Vienna: Politics and Culture* (1980), in which only the early Hofmannsthal appears, while the unfolding fate of modernism and its discontents is represented by the more intransigent Gustav Klimt, Arnold Schoenberg, and Sigmund Freud. For Schorske, the early Hofmannsthal embodies the aesthete's retreat from a political world—and from a world of language, again à la Lord Chandos—in which communication has lost both reason and meaning.

For Schorske, the Austrian fin de siècle follows the defeat of a generation of political liberals and is marked politically by the 1897 election of the outspokenly antisemitic Karl Lueger as mayor of Vienna. On the one hand, this fin de siècle consists of the interior, private world of the symbolist poet Hofmannsthal—the teenage prodigy who wrote under the name "Loris," and, when invited to meet the Viennese literary tastemaker Hermann Bahr, arrived for the appointment dressed in short pants and kneesocks. In a larger context, however, where the personal meets the dynastic and the political, this crisis of *non*recognition is dramatized in the so-called "recognition scene" of *Elektra,* when the returning Orestes and his sister, Elektra, greet each other as strangers. Their crisis is also a crisis of the state. The two dimensions together Schorske called the crisis of the "liberal-rational" order. As for Orestes himself: short of Odysseus, he is perhaps the ur-example of

The Man Who Returned. Post-return, he is menaced by flies (Jean-Paul Sartre, recall, titled his Orestes play *Les mouches*): perhaps a harbinger ghost of the *Palace of Flies*, if reduced in Kappacher's account to the terrace of the Grand Hotel of Bad Fusch in its diminished postimperial state.

The grayly painted death wish of the recumbent Hugo von Hofmannsthal in the summer of 1924 evokes two additional echoes, one on each end of its affective thermometer. On the warm side is Eduard Mörike's glistening 1856 story *Mozart auf der Reise nach Prag* [*Mozart's Journey to Prague*]. On his way to the premiere of *Don Giovanni* in October 1787, the composer and his wife stop to rest at a noble Bohemian estate. Seated at the piano, the composer appears to experience a premonition of his own death. The prose is magical, an apt partner to the idolization of its protagonist. Such romantic writing fades after 1918, and Walter Kappacher stands soberly in that later tradition. Kappacher's sobriety finds an echo in Hofmannsthal's melancholy. No redemption is offered here, neither personal nor historical. In its cool and diagnostic tone, the story absorbs the aura of another Salzburg-raised and identified writer: Thomas Bernhard, whose asceticism, most especially in his five-part memoir, forms a sustained invective (with which another Salzburger, namely Wolfgang Mozart, would have agreed) against his home city's sustained betrayal of its alleged piety and beauty by provinciality and bigotry. Kappacher's protagonist, distinct from the historical figure whose name he bears, recognizes that something enormous has been broken which he cannot fix.

MICHAEL P. STEINBERG's books include *The Meaning of the Salzburg Festival: Austria as Theater and Ideology*, *The Trouble with Wagner*, *The Afterlife of Moses: Exile, Democracy, Renewal*, and a translation of Hermann Broch's *Hugo von Hofmannsthal and his Time*. He is professor of history, music, and German studies at Brown University.

I will show you fear in a handful of dust.
—T.S. ELIOT

*Dedicated to my friends*

On one of the first days, he wondered whether he might have grown too old for this place, which had been a source of conflicted feelings since childhood. Had his memory of the happy days and weeks here, all those years ago, played a terrible trick on him?

What in Bad Fusch was now called the Grand Hotel was, in fact, a third-rate hotel, really an inn but only slightly more distinguished. In earlier days, of course, in the nineties, around the turn of the century, his family and even the more coddled guests of the monarchy's summer resorts had not been as demanding as they were today. Often, they had lodged in the bedrooms of farmers, who in turn slept in the attic during the summer.

Now I have this half-full chamber pot under my bed, it occurred to him, and there is no bell, let alone a telephone, to call Vroni or Kreszenz. Why didn't I stay in Lenzerheide, with dear Carl? The room had been fine, the food first-rate. Swiss, plain and simple: There, the wretched war had not ruined everything. Unlike what he had imagined in Lenzerheide, however, he was as incapable of working in Fusch as he was in Switzerland. Thus far he had been unable to use the undisturbed environment here to his work's advantage.

On the contrary, the best thing here in Fusch had in fact been his acquaintance with Doctor Krakauer, and he very much hoped that it would not break off now—that would be too harsh a punishment for his faux pas. It had been three days since Krakauer disappeared from the face of the earth—on the other hand, he himself had been sitting in his room for the most part, at a little table by the window, unable to believe that his imagination, his associative faculties, had once again completely abandoned him.

He pondered further: Actually, I owe it to my circulatory collapse that I met Krakauer—a wonderful fluke of fate that he happened to pass by!

He would never forget the view through the delicate branches, the radiant crown of the ... beech tree, probably ... tiny veins, the lines of life ... or maple? How the leaves shone, some golden, most green. How many things swept through my head in that moment? Five days it has been—or four?

"It seems to me that you are able to sit up; would you like to try that? I will help you, if I may."

A young man, gray-green loden jacket, held my hand ... apparently counting the beats of my pulse. With the other hand he placed a hat, my hat, in my lap. I had lain on the ground like this once before, some years ago ... in front of a garden gate. In Altaussee, in front of the villa of Baroness ... Lhotsky.

"Are you feeling dizzy?"

The cane the young gentleman was holding was mine. What happened?

"Breathe," he said, "breathe calmly."

An elderly couple in their *tracht*, who had been standing next to the man, now moved away.

He had seen this face once before. Had it been the previous day? If he remembered correctly, in the company of an elderly lady, this man's mother perhaps, wearing a hat with a lavish brim. From some distance, he heard the sound of a postal omnibus's engine revving, struggling up the mountain road.

"Your pulse . . . Allow me."

The young man lowered his voice.

"Herr von Hofmannsthal, isn't it? My name is Krakauer, I'm a physician. Well, your pulse seems to have stabilized. I saw you keel over after passing the stile over there. We brought you to this bench here. Those fine people helped . . . I have a blood pressure gauge in my hotel room . . . It's no wonder! After all, you can almost see the foehn veer into a chilly wind on the ridgeway. That wasn't the case this morning. Stay seated for a moment. If there's anything I can do to help, please just knock on my door at the Hotel Post, room twenty-two.

"Do you suppose you can make it to town by yourself? You wouldn't have very far to go. Take your time, stay seated for a while, Herr von Hofmannsthal. The baroness has gone ahead, we want to change our clothes and take our tea.

3

"She adores you, by the way. The two of you also have a mutual acquaintance—Princess Marie of Thurn and Taxis."

What made him almost cringe at that moment? Was it the princess's bond with Rilke, of which everyone was aware?

"We saw you at the Magenbrünnl yesterday; the baroness immediately recognized you."

Had that been on Monday? In any case, he had eaten with appetite that evening.

An automobile, the engine running at high revs, the exhaust fuming, approached the hotel's forecourt at walking pace. H. paused for a moment on the front steps, looking at the powerful vehicle, its chauffeur in a captain's hat; the car's roof was retracted.

He stepped aside, making room for two gentlemen in long coats with leather caps on their heads who were exiting the hotel. "In this motorist's outfit," he had recently said to Carl, "especially with glasses on—why, I wouldn't recognize even my best friends."

When he finally attempted to enter the hotel foyer, he had to make room once again, for Leo the page, who was carrying two suitcases and had two smaller ones tucked under his arms; he exclaimed, almost croaked, "Good morning, Herr von Hof—." Just in time, the good chap remembered what H. had requested of him, for the second time, one and a half hours ago, when they had met outside, on the road that ran through the village. Leo had been removing weeds from along the wall of the sunroom with a sickle and had yelled . . . —well, he couldn't help himself, and perhaps he had just forgotten that they had already met earlier today. But what striking facial features he had! Unthinkable that this man could pretend to be someone else. Only that his falsetto did not match his bulky skull. H. remembered the kind demeanor his father had perpetually displayed toward servants, and how he, the son, had found it exaggerated here in the mountains, but then ended up adopting it himself. He noticed how a little girl in ragged clothes, a finger up her nose, was watching them both from the other side of the road; evidently the child of some chambermaid or cook. She was standing in front of the entrance to the new hotel, the name of which he had already forgotten.

As he walked up to the reception desk, he remembered that the mail would not arrive until noon, at the earliest. Some resort guests appeared to be leaving. By the seating area in the hall stood a large straw trunk, on which lay two umbrellas.

How old might Leo be? The day H. had arrived in Bad Fusch by postal omnibus—the first time he had not come by oxcart or mail coach—he had been impressed, nay, moved, by the sullen face of Leo, who was dragging the two large trunks from the coach stop to the house, when it suddenly lit up inordinately after he recognized H. in front of the hotel. H. had insisted on carrying his travel bag himself.

"Well, whaddya know, Herr Doktor."

Thank God Leo had not been able to remember his name at that moment. Maybe the reason this impressed me so much, he wondered, was that the house servant didn't know me as a famous writer but only as a summer guest of many years, starting from he was young. His last stay here had been many years ago, though. As he climbed the stairs to his room, he tried to remember: Was it that summer, when Papa could not be stirred to leave Vienna after Mama's death? No . . . the last time he had come to Fusch was in nineteen hundred and eight, that rainy July, the mountain peaks covered in snow, when he had worked here in seclusion, away from his wife and children, on his *Florindo*.

How old might Leo be now? He was struggling a lot to drag the trunks up to his room on the third floor, reminding him very much of Alfons Walde's and Albin Egger-Lienz's maladroit peasant and lumberjack figures.

Now, he would have liked to read about Bad Fusch in the letters of Alexander von Villers, about Sankt Wolfgang, as the village had been called at the time. But the edition's first volume, which he had brought along on his travels, had remained with Carl, who had immediately fallen for the charm of these letters. Villers, he remembered, had said rather disparaging things about Fusch, and had preferred to spend his summers in Ferleiten, at the Lukashansl Inn; he had apparently hiked up to Fusch once a year, or perhaps more often, to experience the goings-on of the resort for a few hours and then feel even better about his stay in Ferleiten. Why hadn't he thought of Ferleiten when he couldn't stand being in Switzerland any longer, when he had pondered where he might be able to lodge during the first half of August, before continuing with his writing in Altaussee, with the family?

In nineteen hundred and nineteen, when he had been so ill, when half of Vienna had been suffering from influenza, he had retreated to Ferleiten at the foot of the Grossglockner mountain, had sat in the kitchen with the innkeepers as their only guest, for three weeks. Did he think himself capable of hiking the Fürstenweg to Ferleiten? One way at most, up to the steep section with the rock steps. It was impossible that Ferleiten would have changed as much as Bad Fusch had in recent years. He could scarcely keep himself from writing to his wife, from telling her how much Bad Fusch had changed, so much so that on his first stroll he'd had a hard time finding his way around all the newly erected buildings and huts. He had almost started to cry from disappointment in his room afterward, which he attributed to exhaustion following the taxing journey. No, Gerty would only worry about him, could conceivably send Christiane to look after him. Gerty was elated, after all, to finally be surrounded by all her children in Aussee, the two boys especially, who would soon be on their way in the world.

I want to get used to all these changes, he resolved. The village road, which had become somewhat wider and, it seemed to him, even dustier, stretched, in the shape of an S, through the tiny hamlet that now was much more densely occupied, the buildings jammed together almost;

hotels, mountain resort, auxiliary structures, a post office, the small shop, even a villa in imperial yellow by the side of the road at the town limits. At the hamlet's center, facing the mountain, somewhat elevated on a plateau, stood the small church unchanged. Behind it, a slightly widened footpath led uphill to the swimming pond and the spring known as the Fürstenquelle. The slope behind the Grand Hotel, which used to be densely wooded, was now completely bare in the lower parts. The steep forest trail to the north lay open; the hike up to the Kreuzköpfl was unquestionably arduous, so exposed to the sun.

*My dear angel, the concierge just handed me a thick bundle with all the mail you have forwarded to me. I'm sitting in the reading room with a few newspapers, waiting until I can repair to the dining room. Last night, they deposited your telegram on my place setting at dinner . . . I was so happy to read that you are merry and well. On a hot day like today, even up here, with the horseflies biting and people lounging by the swimming pond, I am thinking of you, hoping that you are also lying on the lakeshore in Altaussee and going for a swim . . .*

*It was very agreeable in Lenzerheide, dear Carl's concern for me so heartwarming—like a mental asylum attendant, it once crossed my mind . . . You will have received my cards from there by now. Forgive me for not having been able to write a letter. By July, every garret in all of Graubünden has already been booked months in advance. Oh, to be an innkeeper there! The season lasts eight weeks; then they have earned enough to travel to Paris or Cannes. They even cleared out another small garret for me to use as a writing room, put in a table and a large armchair, and brought in a lovely rug from their own apartment. They kept asking whether the food was to my liking—in short, we don't have innkeepers like these in our parts. The parlor maid is very pretty and has good manners. And there's a laundry room in the hallway outside, where an ironer cleaned all the dust stains off my gray suit.*

*Strange that I've never come up to Fusch with you. Maybe—recalling my own childhood days up here—I wanted to spare the children. You, too, would have missed the comfort to which you've grown accustomed.*

*Oh, the joy with which I often think back to our beautiful Italian journey in May, especially Syracuse. I didn't tell you what I had imagined standing at the Fountain of Arethusa: renting a room there and staying the whole summer to work on my* Timon. *You would have had to send me my folders, though, and everything else I'd need . . .*

*Like Isepp said at the Temple of Segesta: Wouldn't you agree that it looked more beautiful from a distance as we were hiking up? Graceful. And now these massive, monumental columns . . . which brought to mind the dainty model of the Ionic temple in the museum in Palermo.*

Yes, proximity, he had thought in Segesta. And: What God could be dwelling here? After all, it is all beyond our capacity to imagine, at least beyond any human measure—and then he had looked around to see what was taking Gerty so long.

*Yet today I thought about discontinuing my stay here in Fusch quite soon and coming to see you in Aussee. I even considered sending you a telegram to see whether all the rooms in our little house are still occupied.*

No, he thought, I can't do that to her. For once, all three children are together, Raimund is going to Berlin in ten days, anyway. That's how long I'll have to bide my time here. For one or two days he would sleep on the sofa in his study in the hut, so that he could still see the boys . . .

Although Carl had advised waiting—after all, it took time for one's system to adjust to Lenzerheide's altitude—he had eventually sent a telegram to the Grand Hotel in Bad Fusch.

Half past eight; he turned on the table lamp. I must, he remembered, write to Gerty that they've also installed electric lights here in the hotels. That the wrought-iron grate inside the church is mostly locked because last year a Baroque statue of the Virgin Mary was stolen. And that the old walkways are partially overgrown with grass or shrubbery. In exchange, they widened the footpath to the swimming pond and the one to the Adolphinen spring.

He pulled the spectacle case out of his frock coat pocket and opened the writing case. So he must have done some work in Lenzerheide after all, he thought, as he held the ink bottle against the lamp. He had to tilt it for his fountain pen to draw ink. He hadn't been able to get any Pelikan ink at his Viennese stationery shop before his departure. The pencils . . . He had lodged many complaints there that the quality of the pencils hadn't been the same since the war; sometimes the writing they produced would become almost illegible merely in a matter of months.

He drew the handkerchief across the backrest of the dilapidated bench. Spiderwebs between the seat slats; he wiped them before putting down his writing case. In the first days of his stay, he had noticed that the resort guests no longer sat on the benches along the walkways but let the waiters serve them on the terraces of the Grand Hotel, the Hotel Post, or the Berghof; there were also fewer benches set up around the village itself. When he sat down, he realized that this was the bench on which he had once sat, even lain, with a book as a headrest, in his childhood and youth. In the past, his parents had always complained that there was never an empty bench to be found on their afternoon strolls, as resort guests sat and chatted everywhere. Only later, at the age of eighteen, had he sometimes been able to socialize with people his own age in Fusch, fun Viennese girls or the young American painter Richard, with whom he had fenced foil. That had been the July with the cold snap, and they had warmed up by fencing daily or sometimes bowling nine-pins at the lane by the swimming pond.

Some of the paths had been widened—especially those that led to various mineral springs—but some others had become overgrown with grass, turned almost invisible. The small village, which had once had only the two hotels and the telegraph office and a few hut-like outposts, had expanded, but his three or four favorite benches were still there. The bench behind the hotel, however, where a steep hiking trail led up the slope, had sunk back into a tilt—when he sat down, he had to struggle to get back up.

During the train ride the other day from Buchs, where Carl had taken him, to Zell am See, he had tried to remember the last time he had gone on a hiking trip from Bad Fusch to Ferleiten.

He opened the book he had with him, a selection of stories by Henry James that his son Raimund had brought from somewhere but evidently not read. On the flyleaf an owner's name had been written in purple ink, Peter Slater. He had taken along this book, with a few others, to Switzerland, because its author was the brother of the psychologist William James, whose works he had long admired. In the middle of the volume, stuck between two pages, was a crushed insect. After breakfast he had lain down on his bed and begun to read the novella *The Lesson of the Master*: "He had been informed that the ladies were at church . . ." It had felt good to be pulled into the story by the author's steady hand. But now he was meant to occupy himself with something different.

It was probably crazy to have come here again; already a mistake, perhaps, to have traveled to Graubünden; the time there with his frien . . . Where? Where to? He was disgruntled by the thought that the summer and fall, the only time when he was able to work continuously, would fly by without yielding fruit due to a poorly chosen setting, due to continuing atmospheric disturbances. He had been irritated in that beautiful Swiss mountain village. Even dear Carl, who had become one of his closest confidants and whom he had been eager to see this summer, Carl, who after long deliberation had suggested Lenzerheide, even Carl had been occasionally difficult to endure this time. What he had liked best was sitting in his hotel room, mulling over his manuscripts or reading Eckermann's *Conversations with Goethe*, which always had a stimulating effect on him. Whenever he had felt he was making no progress with his *Timon*, he had opened the folder with *The Tower*, act five, before going back to *Timon*. His conversations with Carl, to whom he had read quite a bit from the first act, had not been very helpful this time.

Conversely, he had not been able to get the novel *Andreas* out of his head since telling Carl about it at length, weeks ago. Walther Brecht had drawn his attention to Heinse's *Ardinghello*, had even sent him his study on Heinse. Whenever he had been unable to do anything in Lenzerheide, whenever his imagination had been jammed, he had taken notes on a piece of paper for the *Andreas* project. He had long ago realized that the Italian part of his novel was getting out of hand in a way that might ruin the entire book, and yet he kept filling sheet after sheet with excerpts and notes. Perhaps he ought to get serious about his idea of going to Syracuse in late autumn to work on the novel there. To him, Syracuse had been the highlight of their Sicilian journey in the spring, a wonderful birthday present he had given himself. He often became depressed at the thought, one might say the realization, that all three great works might remain fragments, the two plays, the novel.

So, where were we? He took the top two sheets out of the writing case. The outline for *Timon*. It had been Carl's suggestion to briefly summarize everything he had written so far. Based on their conversations about the play, Carl then had noted it all down in his delicate handwriting. As he spent more time looking at these notes, he started feeling almost dizzy. That had been the day before their trip to the Upper Engadine, during which sudden heart troubles had forced them to turn around, giving Carl a terrible fright.

I would need, he thought, someone like Count Harry Kessler, a superior intellect; a few days on retreat with him, as in earlier days with the *Rosenkavalier*, that might invigorate my sluggish ability to make connections. How delighted he had been to receive the letter from Kessler not so long ago, after years of silence. My nerves, he thought, my neurasthenia simply couldn't put up with his stormy temper and his vanities anymore. Even though Kessler was, on top of everything, an eminently political mind, and would surely have been stimulated by the material of this political comedy.

For his *Timon*, he hadn't written anything in Lenzerheide except notes. At least he had read the voluminous book by Robert von Pöhlmann about socialism in antiquity, Carl's copy, and Carl had urged him to pick up a pencil to underline liberally and make notes.

He must have forgotten to wind up his pocket watch in the morning: It said 2:37 p.m., but the afternoon seemed to be well advanced. And he thought about his family, who had been at the house in Altaussee for almost a month now. At all events, he would, before long, be taking pleasure in the familiar surroundings of Aussee, where he would stay well into November, weather permitting. He had always been able to work best in his small room in Aussee.

In the foyer, on the way to the concierge's desk, he happened upon the rotund priest, whom he had seen sitting by himself at a table in the dining room the night before. He returned his friendly nod. As he did so, he remembered that he had to reply to Professor Pauker, the canon of Klosterneuburg— even if the canon had sent him a mere postcard from his Sankt Gilgen summer domicile. Pauker should not be made to think he had forgotten him—after he had campaigned so hard for the *Great World Theater* to be performed, despite continued attacks from an anti-Jewish propaganda rag, in the collegiate church in Salzburg. At first, he had been some-what disappointed that Pauker had not brought his influence to bear with the archdiocese directly. Pauker's article in the *Reichspost*, however, had worked; the archbishop and the cathedral chapter had given in.

"Your mail is here, Herr Doktor . . ." said the concierge overly discreetly; there was no one in their vicinity. "Would you like to take it with you now?" And he ducked behind the counter, put a thick bundle in front of him.

He was hoping it included the book by Marcel Schwob; he had asked his wife to kindly send him the volume from the Oppenheimers' library in Altaussee. These whimsical, very poetic, partly fictional ancient biographies, he thought, might make it easier for him to find his way into the era of *Timon*. A rockslide, the concierge added, had caused the mountain road to be closed indefinitely. The postal driver had dragged the bag from there up to Bad Fusch. He stuck four letters in his pocket and slid the rest of the bundle back to the concierge, telling him he wanted to go for another walk before dinner.

So they still hadn't been able to reinforce the slender mountain road from the Fusch valley to here, in all these years, as they had at the Semmering pass. He remembered how he was supposed to go to Zell am See the year his father had taken ill up here. At the time—it had been the year before his final school examination—the doctor had advised him to walk down to Bruck on foot, about two hours, to take a two-horse carriage from there to Zell am See. But then his father had quickly recovered on his own.

The light rain had stopped, there were glugging sounds everywhere, tiny rivulets on the downward sloping gravel path to the church, water was dripping from the spruces and firs, the barometer was promising a turn for the better. He couldn't walk far, most paths were overgrown with grass, his shoes were not suitable for that. He took the letters out of his frock coat pocket and stopped. Another one from Poldy Andrian; his mind continued going back to his last letter, again and again. How happy he had been that his friend, this man who had spent forever living in solitude, had finally found someone, a wife. And at the same time, he felt uneasy every time he looked at the photograph Poldy had enclosed. This beautiful face seemed to him completely heartless, cold. As a friend he had felt obligated to convey to Poldy his unflinching impression. And he had suggested having the handwriting of his wife-to-be analyzed by a Genevan graphologist Carl had once mentioned to him and whose services he had already used himself. How he hoped that his fears, his premonitions, would prove false.

A little stream was flowing, more forcefully than the thin stream trickling from the iron pipe of the water well into the wooden trough, across the somewhat sunken-in, overgrown stone steps leading up to the church. He sat down on the bench by the church wall. A letter from Carl, one from Richard Strauss, one from Professor Brecht. Brecht would probably thank him for the gift basket of food he had had sent to him and his family on his day of departure in early July. A large ham, fruit, a bottle of wine. And he had also included the first three volumes of his recently published collected works. So many friends and acquaintances had very limited financial means . . . He thought about the two-hundred-dred billion *papiermarks* in his Munich bank account that were now worthless. A few days ago, he had read in the newspaper that the inflation would soon be over, the krone would be replaced by the schilling.

The benches were still damp, but he could just as well do some thinking on foot. In the morning he had gone over the outline Carl had prepared based on their conversations about his *Timon*. He was still convinced that the first act had to open on a square in front of Timon's house. He had a clear idea of the main characters—Timon leading a double life, his son Chelidas, Lycon, and Tryphon—yet when he sat over his writing case, he could not manage to set down a taut, convincing dramatic structure. These characters seemed to him mere templates who couldn't come alive for any true communion in the scenes. But Arthur Schnitzler and Richard Beer-Hofmann had already accused him of this thirty years ago. How often had he studied Shakespeare's and Goethe's dramas and comedies, and Molière, and Grillparzer, too! Actually, from the very beginning he'd had difficulty portraying characters and human destinies effectively on the stage.

He felt a tender yearning, as so often he did when he was alone. *My child, I know how much you wish for me to finally be able to complete* The Tower . . .

He had shaken his head in disbelief when Carl had recently asked whether he couldn't write another play like *The Difficult Man*, set in Austria and in the present-day. So that play had, in fact, remained in Carl's memory, it now occurred to him as he changed his clothes for a walk after breakfast. In one of the pockets of his sports jacket, which he had bought on a whim in Chiavenna on their trip to the south—it had caught his eye in a shop window; he had tried it on and bought it—he found a piece of dried orange peel. Carl had bought two oranges at the market in Soglio, and as they had stood there eating them, he had uttered that sentence about the "Austrian play" . . . The aroma of oranges had taken him back to Syracuse for a moment, where they had tried something in a tavern that he had never heard of: an *insalata di agrumi*, a citrus fruit salad.

Soglio, that enchanting little mountain town . . . He fondly recalled the automobile trip he had taken with Carl ten days ago, and their detour to Chiavenna. The guest book in the Hotel Palazzo Salis in Soglio, where they had found an inscription by Rilke, to whom they had written a postcard after dinner. They had also contemplated visiting Rilke at some other time in his château near Sierre and Sion.

Two women exited the church, conspicuously turned their heads toward him in passing, but did not greet him. If the church was open now, he would take a look inside on his way back.

The afternoon sun had dispersed most of the clouds. He carefully climbed over the stile at the town limits. As he came to the footpath on the meadow, he heard cowbells jingling. Again the notion that he would have to give up his *Timon*, as he had so many things in the past few years. Tie the papers up in a thick folder, strike it from his memory for at least a year. And sometimes the thought to simply quit writing plays, as Sebastian Isepp had done with painting, quit everything altogether, only make notes in his diary. How to make a living? Journalism? Accept the offer from the American publishing group to work as a kind of European correspondent?

He saw a farmer with a pitchfork on his shoulder climbing sideways down the meadow; some distance away, two cows were bolting after him. He stopped, already fearing that the approaching cows or even bulls might gore the man. As soon as they reached the farmer—their farmer, it seemed—they split to amble at his side, one to his left, one to his right.

The slats of the bench with a view of the Embachhorn had dried. He still hadn't found that long flat forest trail he had enjoyed walking as a young man, turning over, in his mind, additional lines for a poem as he walked; he didn't even remember which Fusch forest area this path belonged to. One might reach it by taking the path that led past the Fürstenquelle up to the high Alpine meadows. The trees in this forest had been without branches except very high up; whenever he had walked there, he had felt as if he were in a sprawling cathedral. Now he had to see if he could find the way by approaching it systematically. Twenty-five, thirty-five years it had been—who could say if this forest hadn't since become completely overgrown with erstwhile young spruces and firs. But the paths he took now had to be flat. He could no longer climb the mountains or the steep slopes behind the resort.

As soon as he sat on the bench, he put down his hat and wiped the sweat from his brow and neck with his handkerchief. He resolved to ask Carl in his next letter to bring them a few oranges when he would visit in Aussee in the fall; they had been impossible to get in Vienna for a while now. On the meadow lay leaves blown there by the wind. A bit early, but autumn always began a few weeks earlier up here than down in the valleys. How beautiful, and how strange, the leaves' fine and coarse network of nerves. Had one of the leaves been nibbled by a beetle or a caterpillar? On the ground to his left, he saw a snail's silvery slime trail. It must have been a maple leaf, after all. How perfectly all this was organized, the transport of sap from the roots to the tips of the leaves.

At breakfast he had overheard two German gentlemen in sports jackets at the neighboring table talk about the departure tax. They were around forty years old and looked like twins—how in the world did they end up in Bad Fusch? He had heard that this tax could be as high as twenty *goldmarks*. As a Swiss citizen, Carl would have a much easier time entering Austria, thank God.

The fourth day in Fusch. As he strolled around with abandon, stopped at a well, and bent down to drink, for a moment he thought himself in ghostly company: He saw himself twenty, thirty or more years ago walking around here alone, drafting lines of a poem, reciting poetry.

How many poems, he thought, did I know by heart back then? Many verses by Nikolaus Lenau, some of which he still remembered:

> If you've seen fortune pass you by
> Never to be found again
> Just lend a creek your weary eye
> Where all things sway and wane . . .

That summer, when the poems came to mind as if by themselves . . . Once, while walking without a pencil at hand, he had memorized two terze rime over and over so they wouldn't vanish as quickly as they had appeared. Mourning the death of Frau von Wertheimstein had bathed everything in a wistful light. That she would soon expire had been clear to him after his last visit in Döbling. Franziska Gomperz's telegram, which arrived just as he and his parents were about to leave Vienna for their summer retreat, had affected him deeply.

He opened Gerty's letter: one sheet from her and a letter Rudolf Borchardt had written to Christiane. How he loved his wife's handwriting; he kept all these notes in his wallet.

Who was it that the young man—whom he had encountered for the second time at the town limits, where the road forked into two walking paths that also branched off after a while—reminded him of? He was on his way back from a short morning hike to the Augenquelle, a spring said to heal the eyes, where, seated on a bench with the Pinzgau High Tauern mountain range in front of him, he had taken some notes on his writing pad. Opposite the church he sat down once again, on another bench, in the middle of the circle formed by six mighty chestnut trees. Suddenly he remembered what he had written down last week in Lenzerheide: insert a scene with a hetaera into his *Timon*, based on Diotima's speech in Plato's *Symposium*. He wanted to call Gerty in Aussee in the evening, to tell her that he would need his Plato as soon as he moved with all his writing gear to Altaussee.

The young man with his strikingly short haircut had come from the Kasereckweg, that steep path zigzagging down, which he had often hiked up in his younger years, several times each year, usually with his father. Afterward, milk and buttered bread at the Riedelalm. Apparently, this boy, too, had come up here with his parents. Last night in the hotel's dining room, he had observed the family seated in the back. All three individuals at the table had seemed familiar to him, especially the middle-aged gentleman. But when he had finally found his glasses, they had already left their table.

He had been to the church consecrated to Bishop Wolfgang of Regensburg, in which he had sat devoutly as a child; the many burning candles rendered the narrow interior a cave in which one enjoyed settling down. Sometimes he would slip a few hellers into the slot of the heavy iron box, take a candle, light it with a burning one, and stick it on an empty spike. And then wish that the rain would stop, that his mother would get better, that he would find the paperback of d'Annunzio essays that he had left on some bench or had inadvertently dropped somewhere the day before. Or that he would write a successful poem . . . Two days ago, he had lit another candle here, after all these years, and hadn't known what to wish for; when two people had entered, he had felt embarrassed holding the burning candle in his hand, and had stuck it on the candle rack, made the sign of the cross, and left the little church. This time he saw a young man in knee breeches and woolen stockings kneeling and praying in the rearmost pew. The gate in the tall wrought iron grate was open. Was he allowed to wish for his work, his writing, to go smoothly? Why not? The things people ask for in church! Mounted on the left wall was a horrendously tasteless picture of the Virgin Mary. Muslim aniconism—one might wish for that in some instances. How much was one supposed to give now? He remembered a sentence, where had he read it? The only reason the gods are not present is that nobody called upon them . . . He took a few bills from his wallet, one thousand five hundred kronen, that ought to be enough, and lit a candle. It took awhile for the wick to light. Now the young man rose, looked at him, stopped, as if he also wanted to donate a candle, nodded goodbye, and left the church. Finally he stuck the candle on one of the spikes and thought about how to formulate his wish.

On the very first evening in the dining room, he had noticed some guests were not wearing evening attire at their tables. He, too, had brought just a dark dinner jacket for the evenings on his trip to Switzerland. Carl had pointed out to him that nowadays—except in the most extravagant hotels—one dressed casually for the summer. Sitting at a table here now was a gentleman wearing a white shirt and a most preposterous necktie. Scarcely anyone accompanying his lady to the table pulled out her chair. He knew the large-scale picture on the wall, a view of the Grossglockner mountain with its mighty Pasterze glacier, from his past stays; if he recalled correctly it used to hang in the hall. The waiters seemed clumsier than before the war, twice in the past few days he had seen them drop a plate or cutlery. The gueridon or tea trolley they pushed through the dining room rattled and banged into tables; the waiters seemed to lack a sense of the space in which they moved. There was nothing to fault about the food, however; yesterday's calf's liver with buttered rice, boiled potatoes, and beans had been exquisite. For dessert, they had served fruit and Emmental cheese—which he had never had in Lenzerheide. It had become loud in the hotels, even in Lenzerheide, barely anyone lowered their voice, boisterous laughter at night, doors slamming, giggling in the corridors . . . He had also contemplated telling the concierge that he did not like the taste of their coffee. Hogweed, mullein, and coltsfoot had sprouted up at the stairs to the entrance. He had also noticed some of the guests wearing ordinary low shoes on their hikes instead of mountaineering boots.

And he thought about his family in Aussee again. How he had mourned the loss of the house in Obertressen number fourteen, where they had lodged during so many summer and autumn months. Sometimes, while strolling around, he would feel a sudden stabbing pain in his heart, until he remembered that they had another house, after all, not even that far from the previous one. The summer before, the farmer's wife had put in front of him not just the daily can of milk but also a basket of eggs, bacon, and a loaf of bread before proceeding to explain in a roundabout way that her husband would soon come to talk to him: Starting next spring, they would need the house for themselves, the son wanted to get married . . .

The prospect of no longer having a house in Aussee the next summer and autumn had depressed him for weeks; he'd had to interrupt his work on a ballet scenario and instead read his edition of Pedro Calderón's plays looking for possible adaptations. Even if they found another house in Altaussee, he thought at the time, it wouldn't necessarily be a house in which he could live, or in other words, work. And how far might that dwelling be, then, from his favorite bench! Sometimes, when the two boys made too much of a racket, he would take his writing case and walk to the bench at the edge of the forest. When it was empty, he felt at one with the world. This bench, he would sometimes think, my real home. They had been lucky with the new house, the mayor had helped them procure it. But he had grown so used to hanging his hat on the roe antlers when returning from a stroll that, whenever he stepped into the similarly dark hallway, he would stretch up his arm, hat in hand, to remember only too late that it was now their umbrellas that hung from the long protruding wooden nails.

He reached for his notebook and jotted down the sentence that he had just read in a French newspaper, a selection of notes by Paul Valéry: "A plagiarist is a man who has badly digested what he has got from others." While reading, it occurred to him that over the years, critics had made a habit of calling him a plagiarist or an epigone. As if not everybody learned from one's predecessors, was inspired by the masters. As if it were not important, after all, to make something original from all these inspirations. It was late. He hadn't been able to write a single line that day either; nor had he seen Krakauer, the young physician.

The true art form, he thought, was to look for the right tone in a great master, to buttress oneself with that tone and then to make one's own ... How upset his friend Eberhard von Bodenhausen had been when, years ago, he thought he had detected Goethe's tone in a short essay of his. Yes ... Whenever the first sentence in a prose work showed no desire to emerge, when nothing worked, he liked to pick up the volume of Goethe's essays on art theory. The *Introduction to the Propylaea* had often been helpful to him. "A young man who feels attracted to art and nature expects, by striving vigorously, to gain immediate entrance to the inner sanctum. As an adult he discovers that after a long and arduous pilgrimage he is still in the vestibule." A few sentences sufficed to put himself on solid ground. To arrive at a tone required firm terrain under one's feet.

Finding a tone, on the other hand, one's own tone, and then sounding that same tone again and again like George and also Rilke ... How he sometimes envied Schnitzler for the continuity of his work! How Wedekind's light touch had helped him in earlier days, he remembered, to find the right tone for his adaptation of *Venice Preserv'd* ... He still missed his father; he had sometimes trusted his wise judgment more than that of the professional critics. The somnambulistic certainty of the early years, when almost everything turned out right . . . The conversations with his father in his younger years, in the cool, rainy summer days up here and then in Strobl. Reading to him . . . How sharply Papa had reacted when in Fusch H. once let him read a letter he had just written to Stefan George recommending that a few poems by his friend Poldy be included in the *Blätter für die Kunst*. "What kind of tone are you using there!" his father had exclaimed. "One doesn't just change one's tone!" At the time he had sometimes wondered whether he even had a tone of his own; upon his return home after that long first summer in Aussee, his father had criticized his tone of voice: It was unbearable, he had said. Well, I talk like all my friends talk, he had thought, like Felix Oppenheimer, Poldy Andrian, Clemens, Georg Franckenstein. They had all exchanged his letters, read them, and read them to one another, and they had admired him for striking an individualized personal tone with each of his addressees. But, and of this he was sure, if he hadn't already been a renowned artist in Viennese circles at the time, they would never have let him get as close to them as he had; to them he was no man of the world.

While cleaning his teeth, he resolved to knock on Doctor Krakauer's door the next day, to invite him to coffee in the salon.

Someone to talk to, he had increasingly gone without that, and it became correspondingly harder to put up with idle chatter. He let Hans-Karl say in his play *The Difficult*

*Man* that the most awful thing was that there was such a thing as conversation, the tattle that flattened every exchange. He enjoyed listening to the farmers, the roadmen, even the housekeeper in Aussee or Rodaun—when he had the time, of course, or was in the mood, or wasn't at that moment in some other world—but the prattle of the so-called cultured people! Drifting apart from Richard Beer-Hofmann, also Schnitzler... Poldy, always difficult, and abroad most of the time... seemed to have wholly surrendered to the Catholic Church to boot. Rudolf Pannwitz, in whom he had placed such high hopes. His *Crisis of European Culture* had, when the author had sent it to him during the war, illuminated his life. In those difficult months, when he had felt unable to get over the collapse of the empire—to him this meant the eradication of all existence. What hadn't he done to help this genius who lived nearby in abject poverty! Collected money. Procured him a longer stay in the house of a friend, Countess Ottonie Degenfeld, in Bavaria. And then this man conducted himself so terribly indecorously. He had already been living with two women anyway! How strange that was: Either one found the work of a man whom one did not like personally very meaningful, or the other way around.

When Ottonie had informed him of the downright embarrassing incident in a letter, he had felt a rage rising within. His horror, had this Pannwitz fellow pressured Gerty, would not have been greater. Ottonie... how smitten I have been with her at times, he thought. At least he still had the epistolary conversations with her. His wife had once said that his letters on their own were more than most authors ever accomplished.

What time was it? At all events, he had missed the two o'clock postal bus. He would have liked to stroll around the alleys of Zell am See, to look for a gift for his wife that he would bring her in Altaussee. He looked forward to being alone with Gerty—and hopefully the weather would hold— to then work in familiar surroundings well into November. When he was away from home, he often felt a fierce tenderness for her, and then, at home, that affection waned. It was difficult to buy something for her, he had always preferred it if she picked something for herself.

He rearranged the sheets from his writing case. It was probably Doctor Krakauer who had collected them and put them in there after his fall the other day. Except for some notes on *Timon* he hadn't managed to write anything that day, much like the day before. On his way home he had said to himself: How absurd to have come here. I should have stayed in Switzerland. Perhaps I would have been able, after Carl's departure, to get some work done in Lenzerheide after all.

Drink tea! A cup of good tea . . . But you did not get that here. Not anymore. In Lenzerheide you did, a paradise when it came to coffee, tea, and pastries.

As he had lain on the bench on Monday after his fall, half-unconscious, he had felt something pulling him away— where to? Then he had awoken, had admired the lush foliage of the beech tree above him. Maybe something had pulled him in there. He would get into such states in his younger years... How did the lines in the terze rime go?

> And know that life placidly flows
> From their somnolent limbs
> To the trees and grass...

The handrail of the small bridge across the creek—a pole was missing, the handrail shaky—that's where it had started. Then the long, tall, crooked log pile by the creek, secured to a spruce by a chain—he was still afraid every time that the colossal pile might come loose and bury him as he passed by. Evading it would be impossible, because the narrow path was bordered by a steep embankment on the other side.

The scares yesterday and today... those ghosts! Or was he becoming senile? Yesterday, when his skull had been on the verge of bursting due to the warm winds, when he had been sitting on the terrace after breakfast reading the *Neue Freie Presse*, once again considering telegraphing Gerty to ask whether his room was already vacant, whether Franzl had perhaps already returned to Vienna, he had suddenly seen that gentleman approaching him. Why, if that isn't Rudolf Borchardt, he surmised, and it gave him a terrible chill. Had he come to discuss—settle—our conflict over the *Eranos* volume? The evening before, he had perused Borchardt's translation of Walter Savage Landor's *Imaginary Conversations* again and read parts of it; after all, that was a genre he himself had worked and published in. That evening he had noted down an idea for a made-up conversation: *Friends*.

That slender, almost dark-skinned face of the gentleman who stood at his table and asked in the most exquisite Viennese accent whether the *Neue Freie Presse* on his table was available. He was so relieved that he handed the gentleman the newspaper, clamp and grip first, "Oh, please go ahead!" How incredibly stupid to think that a deeply offended Rudolf Borchardt might turn up here in Bad Fusch! Now he noticed that it was a disabled veteran with an artificial right arm and a hand fashioned from black leather. In the dining room, one also saw men moving about on crutches. New guests, the concierge had told him, would arrive the next day; he hoped that none of their faces would be familiar.

Two days ago, when he had handed the concierge some letters to frank and had been looking through the list of guests at the far end of the reception desk, he had heard a man his age ask for Herr Hofmannsthal. He had turned around and hurried up the stairs. Right then he remembered how he had once fled—totally absurdly—from Rilke at the Vier Jahreszeiten in Munich, where he had also been staying. For a few days they had exchanged brief correspondence regarding a meeting that ended up not taking place, because they could not agree on an hour. When in the evening he had stepped out of his room and locked it, Rilke had been at the end of the corridor walking toward him in the company of, and in conversation with, a tall lady, and he had been so startled that he pulled open the door of the floor's storeroom and waited there in darkness for a few minutes. On his first day in Fusch, he had looked around the dining room and had been relieved to see that apparently the Brechts had not come, after all. For the time being, he would have felt extremely uncomfortable if he'd had to subject himself to conversation twice or thrice a day or been obliged to take a postprandial stroll in the company of others.

Ever since the publication of the *Eranos* Festschrift, he had been disappointed in Walther Brecht. Brecht had written his contribution about him, the honoree, clearly while uninspired and in haste. Some sentences had left him shaking his head, and he had suddenly realized he could not count on Professor Brecht for the fundamental study of his work that they had discussed several times in Vienna. Too easy to praise *Everyman* and the *Rosenkavalier*. He had almost regretted having provided Brecht with the manuscript containing the diary-like notes he had made over the years. On the other hand, Brecht had often been very stimulating in conversation, strangely less so when he visited him in Rodaun and more so during brief fortuitous encounters when they happened upon each other in the streets of Vienna. He had brought Brecht's book about Wilhelm Heinse and had read parts of it in Lenzerheide, parts of the novel *Ardinghello* as well, torn between ardor and repulsion. Remarkable, it seemed to him, how deeply Heinse was able to delve into the Mediterranean way of life.

Back in the village he passed the hotel, saw some people sitting on the terrace having coffee, stopped on the bridge, where the Weixel stream shot down from the mountain in its deeply carved bed at the gloomy back of the building, swollen by the rain of the previous day. He stood on the bridge, submitting to the water's roar for a while, turned around, took a few steps, looked downstream into the frothing flow. Surely, nobody could survive that jump.

A long honking sound startled him; he hadn't seen or heard the postal bus coming, and the driver honked a second time. Yes, of course, he had to get off the bridge, it was too narrow, not easy for the driver to cross. That meant the blocked road down to the Fusch valley had been cleared again.

What might the mailman have for him today? He hadn't even read all of yesterday's letters yet. He would have to confirm the one from Richard Strauss regarding *The Egyptian Helen* soon, as he would the one from Poldy; but replying to each and every letter at length like he used to do was impossible.

On the bench at the edge of the forest he had been able to immerse himself in his shadow realm, in the company of his larval characters, who strove more or less to take shape, to acquire contours, to be brought to life ... As he had worked on his new play sometimes the strangest company appeared to him; nobody could ever really imagine what kinds of people one rubbed shoulders with. Underneath the characters' masquerades one got very close to so many bygone and dreamt-of things, so much that had vanished and been yearned for, so many things one had never possessed ... Letting a voice, a

character appear—that of *Timon*—creating tension, building a scene, other characters ... Weren't even the deepest
states of our inner lives, he thought, strangely connected
with a landscape, with atmospheric conditions?

He had noted, jotted down some thing, he had tried out
dialogues, and thank God, he had remained undisturbed on
his bench. What should he think of the fact, he thought, that
when he had finally opened his puppet theater, as he called it,
on that marketplace in Athens, he would remember the dialogue, eyes closed, and suddenly Basilius and Julius from *The
Tower* would come creeping in ... Did that mean he ought
to give in, tie up the *Timon* folder with a string and transport
himself from third-century Greece to the fictitious mythical
age of *The Tower*? He pondered whether he had in that folder
the seven handwritten pages on which he had sketched the
play's structure and plot many years ago, when he had set out
to translate Calderón's play.

The concierge waved at him with a pouch as he entered the
hotel. The afternoon mail. He tore open the first envelope
with his index finger, took it to the reading room, and hoped
to be able to deal with—by which he meant throw away—
part of the mail right here, downstairs. Gerty was never quite
sure what was important to him, so she also forwarded letters from people she did not know, just in case, letters from
readers, queries, messages from the publisher, etc. She had
enclosed a letter Frau Brecht had written to her. A month
ago, in a weak moment, he had recommended Bad Fusch to

Professor Brecht, who had asked him about a summer retreat. The Brechts now claimed that they hadn't been able to get a room. That was just as well. But maybe it was an excuse, because there were enough vacancies in Fusch this year, he himself had been able to choose between three different ones. He sat down in the armchair by the window, shielded by tall potted plants. A letter from Carl: *Are you still in Fusch, I wonder? Have you found a quiet place to work, does much joy come from your memories, or are you nostalgic about your early years...? I have been in Zurich since that Sunday I drove you to Buchs. The Zurich library has always been a favorite work space of mine...*

Am I becoming totally incapable, the older I get, of being together with people, even friends, for longer than a day or two or three? A letter from Poldy Andrian, problematic as always, and one from Paul Zifferer, who was spending the summer in Austria; he'd also had to withdraw from this stalwart friend. Zifferer had helped him a lot in matters of Parisian theater—above all, to save a great deal of money—but he had been unable to receive Zifferer, neither in Salzburg nor in Fusch, nor had he wished to. He did not know what he would do if this summer, this fall, he weren't able to either make progress on *Timon* or bring *The Tower* to completion. At least the second, the third, and the fifth act of *The Tower* were presentable now, and he had even thought about to whom he should send one of the acts for an advance printing. One more folder with a fragmented bundle of papers? The number of his finished works was by far surpassed by the number of folders containing ones he had given up on.

Ria Claassen complained that she had not received the Salzburg Festival program. He could not possibly inform hundreds of people there would be no festival this year, and why. Least of all the reasons reported by the press: because an actress had canceled, or for lack of money... The main cause, much rather, was the catastrophic situation throughout the country, the rising currency devaluation. Food shortages, housing scarcity, and unemployment were causing local residents great hardship, they could not be receptive to the idea of a festival. Here and there, there had already been protests against it in Salzburg. A certain reactionary press was stirring the pot. In any case, there was concern that festively dressed visitors arriving from all over Europe and even overseas would be harassed by the locals in front of the festival hall.

Couldn't he pay the hotel bill by check? Otherwise, he would somehow have to drag the paper currency from the bank in Zell am See all the way here in his little suitcase. Should I, he pondered, suggest that Ottonie come here and then I'd go with her to Aussee?

*My dearest creature, I just dropped off a few letters at the post office, and the two elderly women in front of me at the counter were talking about marriages of convenience, how they were preferable to marriages of love. I often think about how happy I am with you—so ours, too, would be a marriage of convenience, wouldn't it? I just remembered today that you have never been to*

*Fusch. Before we got married, our families each had gone their own ways in summer, and later I went to Fusch alone, to work and only to work . . . Everything has changed a lot here and at the same time hasn't changed at all. Much has been built, there are four hotels now, they have all had electric lighting since last year, but there is still one kerosene lamp in each room, because power outages are quite frequent. I'm afraid Carl wasn't too happy with me. On an outing in the automobile, I felt sick, my heart, we had to turn around . . .*

No, he could not write her that.

*Time and again, I've written you letters in my thoughts on my strolls, and in the evening, in my room, I thought I had really written to you . . .*

*Unfortunately, they say that the weather will soon take a turn. Well, that dreadful inheritance from my mother . . . my physical disposition, my dependence on the quality of the air, my dreadful sensitivity to weather . . . But you've already known that for twenty-five years. You were right, of course, my harsh reaction to Rudolf's essay was disproportionate, as was my reaction to Josef Nadler's article. You know, I brought the volume with me and read some of the things again in Lenzerheide. I always ruin it with people who have been good to me and my concerns.*

*Let's go traveling for three months for my sixtieth, yes?*

*Is someone currently lodging on the Ramgut estate? I wrote to Yella Oppenheimer from Switzerland but so far haven't received a reply. I did invite Carl to come to Aussee in September. There'll be room for all of us; if not, I'll ask Yella for my little room again. Could Christiane go up to the library and see if they have Plato's major works, at least* The Symposium? *Didn't I read that beautiful speech of Diotima to you once? And maybe Lucian's hetaerae dialogues? I would need these two for my* Timon. *Otherwise I'd have to have someone send me my things from Vienna. I'm not working just yet, not really, you know how it is, the constant ups and downs of the imagination . . . sometimes this deceptive abundance, then a period of ebb . . . But do not worry: Whenever I can't work, I'll put a book in my pocket and stroll over to a bench. You know that since time immemorial I've had a bench with a table where I write, at the foot of a steep mountain meadow. Whenever I wanted to pause and sit down with someone to talk during a stroll (in earlier days, now there's nobody I know here who knows me anymore), I always chose a different bench.*

The waiter in the tearoom came back and informed him that he was sorry but it was currently impossible to find the *Neue Freie Presse* anywhere. A guest must have taken it to his room again. He handed Herr Egon the *Journal* and the *Salzburger Volksblatt* and asked him to put the tea on his hotel bill.

The news of Joseph Conrad's death had unsettled him: "The 67-year-old Polish-British writer died of heart failure August 3rd." He recalled that Kafka had also died this year, and last week the composer Ferruccio Busoni. Conrad had long been a novelist he admired. Last winter he had read *The Secret Agent*. He remembered well what he had thought at the time: Yes, this is how a novel should be written; you have to physically feel the author's presence between the lines as you read them.

On the train ride from Buchs to Bad Fusch, he had read the afterword of a story collection by Henry James and learned that James and Conrad had lived only twenty kilometers from each other in southern England, that they visited each other and exchanged letters. That had saddened him, because it had made him realize he had had no colleague in Rodaun, not even in Vienna, with whom he could meet, with whom he could really talk. He had drifted apart from Beer-Hofmann—an unrequited love—and his meetings with Schnitzler had also grown fewer since the war. Still, more than them, he missed talking to his father. Perhaps precisely because his father was not a writer . . .

"I don't want to interrupt . . . good afternoon."

"You're not interrupting at all."

It was Doctor Krakauer. H. arose.

"I was just about to get up. I simply must go to the post office to drop off a few letters so they can be dispatched."

Krakauer asked if he might join him and how he was feeling today. Baroness Trattnig was here, he said, getting a health treatment for her frayed nerves.

"Her niece, Elisabeth von Trattnig, is keeping her company. You see, I am currently in the service of the baroness, as her private physician, so to speak. She travels a lot, has money, a lot of money, her husband lost his life two years ago in a train accident in Czechoslovakia, perhaps you remember the newspaper report. She was my patient at the Vienna General

Hospital. And working there did not suit me. Without much deliberation, I accepted her offer to accompany her, to be her private physician. She is a bit . . . possessive, but I know how to defend myself."

They crossed the foyer. A gentleman in a trench coat sat in an armchair surrounded by luggage, glancing at them with suspicion.

"Apparently, they only have the *Wiener Journal* here," H. said to Krakauer, "or someone is hogging the *Presse*," and invited him with a gesture of his arm to accompany him.

"The *Journal*," he added, "is currently printing a serial novel on its last page. The daily recapitulation today starts like this: 'The famous sculptor Rudolf Kerr has fallen in love with the Russian Princess Tatyana Kengarin . . .'—or something to that effect. Do you know anyone who would read a thing like that?"

"But of course," Krakauer replied, "the whole world does. It's always been that way. You know as well as I that even the so-called upper classes read E. Marlitt's novels or the like, and of course the serializations in the appropriate magazines."

As they walked along the gravelly path, passing the resort building and the pharmacy, H. told Krakauer that for years he'd been having dreams of walls, the walls of rooms, no, set walls like in a theater play, closing in as he lay there, eventually threatening to crush him; so far he'd always awakened in time . . . Last night there had been another power outage; how fortunate that there was a kerosene lamp in every room.

"Until my marriage," he continued, "I'd spent every summer since childhood in Bad Fusch with my parents. July in Bad Fusch, which was especially good for Mama, who suffered from neurasthenia, and then, in late July, we relocated to Strobl am Wolfgangsee...

"I just met with a friend, a Swiss man, in Graubünden; he, by the way, worked as an attaché in Vienna for several years after the war, Carl Jacob Burckhardt. I wanted to finish writing a play, or at least get very far with it, in the three weeks there in Lenzerheide. But as opportune as that beautiful place and the excellent hotel had seemed for my endeavors upon my arrival, so distraught was I after the first week... A place devoid of any spirit, if you can imagine what I mean. The elevation was right—perhaps a bit too high for me, almost one thousand five hundred meters above sea level, I know from experience that about one thousand would be ideal—Bad Fusch is about twelve hundred. The weather was pleasant but my imagination was blocked, I could not do anything. As it was impossible to find my way into the play I was working on, not by day, nor by night, my mind returned to an old novel project. But what am I talking about..."

They had reached the small post office. He pulled a few letters from his frock coat pocket and slipped them into the box next to the entrance.

"Fortunately," he said to Krakauer, "the barometer does not show inauspicious conditions today, much better than yesterday; we might get good weather still, in the next days."

42

He aired his hat; his scalp was itching. "When you're young, you know...A rainy summer is irksome. How often have I experienced them, especially here in Bad Fusch. But I could still write poems even in low atmospheric pressure. But now...One grows more impatient the older one gets."

He stopped, stepped to the side with Krakauer, three summer guests were approaching, walking side by side, none of them made attempts to make way.

"The number of years one still has ahead grows smaller and smaller: One bungled summer, and possibly more continuous rain in autumn, quickly turns into a disaster. Sometimes, many years ago now, I wondered whether it wouldn't have been wiser to quit writing at the age of twenty, like my friend Baron von Andrian and become a civil servant or give lectures at university."

"But you're not old yet," Krakauer objected. "You are in the prime of life, surely you will go on to write many great things yet. If only I could help...If we were in Vienna, I would recommend a visit to Chief Physician Sonnleithner, one of the most eminent cardiologists. I would insist that you—pardon me—let him give you a thorough examination. You should also have your eyes..."

H. replied that he had already had problems with his sight in his youth: "Yet it is right here in Fusch that we have the famous Augenquelle with healing waters for the eyes. Have you ever been there? One has to go through the ravine, the gloomy path down the right-hand side of the hotel, past the grocer...Well, I always walked to the Augenquelle twice a day, sprinkled my eyes, in the morning and again after dinner, and I've never had troubles with my eyes in Fusch. I ought to try it now... All those letters—because of work I always neglect everything else, anyway... I'd probably need a separate trunk for all the things that pile up, the letters, newspapers, books... But humans are strange creatures: Only two letters arrived yesterday, and I didn't like that either. I wondered what was wrong—whether the world had forgotten me."

Krakauer said that he had spent eight years in the United States, that he had started his studies at Columbia University. His father had forbidden him to come home in nineteen hundred and seventeen, as long as the war was still going on—his older brother had fallen in Romania, he said.

"I graduated in nineteen hundred and eighteen, and actually wanted to return to Vienna. Originally, I had wanted to stay only two years at the most, but I liked life in Manhattan so much, I was impressed by the generosity and openness of people there. When I returned after the war, I had trouble getting my bearings. Suddenly everything seemed so lifeless and diffuse, even vicious. The hurdles before I received formal recognition of my foreign academic degree to finally be able to practice medicine in Austria."

H. said he had written an epistolary story many years ago, *The Letters of the Man Who Returned.* He offered to lend him the recently published volume in which this text appeared.

They reached the hotel.

"How I would love to finally read something you have written!" Krakauer exclaimed.

H. replied that he would leave the volume with the concierge.

"Unfortunately," he said, "I left my lemon balm tincture at the hotel in Lenzerheide. But I want to go down to Zell am See for a few hours today or tomorrow, anyway."

He wanted to add that in Zell am See he hoped not to see Herr Windhager, the owner of the Seehotel, who had become the president of the Ferdinand Raimund Society after the war; this respectable gentleman had already asked him several times for an essay about Raimund . . .

Suddenly a heavyset lady in her fifties blocked his path, a wide-brimmed white hat on her head.

"Herr von Hofmannsthal! What an honor to meet you. Two years ago, I saw the *Great World Theater* in this church in Salzburg—wonderful, just wonderful! We had hoped to experience your *Everyman* this summer . . ."

"Pleased to hear that," he mumbled and pushed past the lady.

"Sebastian! Where have you been? Didn't we want to . . . we still have two suitcases at the Hotel Post!"

H. turned around to find Krakauer, who now extended his arm toward the lady—evidently, it was his baroness. Sebastian? That reminded him of Sebastian Isepp again, of their Italian journey in the spring . . . A plump young woman nearby also seemed to be part of the baroness's retinue, it must have been the singer. She handed the baroness a small box or something from her purse.

How impolite of me again, it struck him, how very

impolite. But if there was one thing he could not stand—
could stand less and less—it was all these ladies who often
reminded him of his mother-in-law. Gerty had come to
resemble her, but that was different. And yet he pondered,
what would I be, what would we be . . . ? Without them, after
all, every auditorium would be half-empty . . . And who reads
the most books after all? Krakauer turned around to find
him, seemed to want to give him some sort of sign. In the
foyer, the concierge waved to him discreetly.

"A telegram for you, Herr . . . "

The good man had remembered that H. had asked him
not to utter his name.

Though those days were long past and gone . . . In
Germany, maybe. But in Vienna? Who in the world knew
him there? While he was climbing the stairs, he remembered
a comment by the author Marie von Ebner-Eschenbach, who
at an advanced age complained to Ferdinand von Saar that
people had completely forgotten her. It was ridiculous, but it
still aggravated him when he recalled that no public authority in Vienna—not even in Rodaun—had sent him birthday
wishes in February, let alone awarded him a decoration. Poor
Saar, severely ill, had killed himself at an old age.

He stopped and searched all his frock coat pockets for a
pencil; he must have left it in his room. Will I remember,
he thought, to ask Christiane to go and get me some lemon
balm tincture in Bad Aussee as soon as possible? He didn't
feel like walking all the way to the cabin today, where they

served the best *schwarzbrot* and the best buttermilk and the
most delightful butter-fried doughnuts. Only another quarter
of an hour, maybe twenty minutes—but there was the long
way back to the village to keep in mind. As he was wiping
the sweat off his forehead with his handkerchief, he suddenly
remembered whom Krakauer's baroness reminded him of . . .

He turned around and looked at the mountain ridges in
the west, then down into the Fusch valley, then over to the
village. He could not make out the gables of the hotel buildings and auxiliary structures from where he was. Why had he
not realized on the first two days how much this hamlet had
expanded? Only now did he take note of all the new buildings along the main road, which bent westward leading out
of the village. He did not have a long way to go to the bench,
which yielded a beautiful view of the jagged massif of the
Schwarzkopf, almost three thousand meters in height, whose
peak was often covered in snow, sometimes even in summer.

He remembered his encounter with Baroness Lhotsky
in that awful year nineteen hundred and nineteen, in
Altaussee . . . Strange, he had experienced a dizzy spell that
time as well. And the baroness's servant, who may have been
weeding along the fence in the estate's garden, had noticed,
apparently, how he had grabbed the fence post before
collapsing.

It had been on the Lhotskys' terrace that he had regained
consciousness. The baroness had served him tea in her salon
and had apologized that there had been no coffee to buy.
And, as the chair of the Salzburg Festival association, had

reminded him that he had promised the festival's president, Richard Strauss, to write an advertisement text.

Well, the things you promise, he had thought.

She had been unable to reach him, for months, the baroness had called out, what a coincidence now... People had expected him to be in Aussee, without a telephone line. Or down with the flu.

He had indeed been ill a long time, he had replied. Thank God, he had thought, that we don't have one of those importunate devices in our little house in Altaussee. In Rodaun, there was a telephone on the ground floor next to the kitchen that was operated by the maidservant.

Would he not please... there was a typewriter on the premises... He had not responded to the president's two dispatches. It would be only a few lines, after all, it was mainly about putting his name...

He had instantly remembered then that he had sat at the curved cherrywood desk once before, it may have been twenty years ago. Longer than that, he had ruminated, it had been his first summer in Aussee, in eighteen eighty-six. He had met Major Lhotsky and his wife at a dinner hosted by the Oppenheimers at the Ramgut estate, and he, the universally celebrated young poet, had been invited to tea at the Lhotsky villa some weeks prior, together with his friend Clemens Franckenstein, who had proceeded to play pieces from his opera *Griseldis* on the piano, although the guests' applause had remained rather restrained. At the time, he had secretly observed the attractive baroness; she had been only a few years older than him and, unlike today, had not dressed like a local in a dirndl and rose-colored silk scarf.

While she laboriously poured his tea into a cup and then fiddled with her shawl, he remembered how he had shaken his head one morning, saying his goodbyes to Gerty and the children, who had wanted to go on a tour in the Totes Gebirge and had planned to stay overnight at the Brunnwiesenalm. Christiane, pretty to look at as always, in her dirndl costume and with her rucksack, but the boys in lederhosen already a few sizes too small, the green kneesocks and felt hats, with their walking canes . . . But then he had remembered, on his stroll, that he had had the same gear at that age.

"I will write something nice in your guest book," he had told the baroness, "but now I'd have to . . . The festival idea and the Salzburg Festival are dear to my heart, everybody knows that, and you do, too. After all, it is the best and only thing that I can do now, after the collapse of the empire, for the Austrian, the European idea. Raimund, Goldoni, Mozart, Schubert . . . Surely you know that I have published several articles on this subject. Well, the cathedral chapter," he had added, "has finally, at least verbally, given its approval for *Everyman*."

If only people would stop constantly asking him for something! What were they thinking, five pages here, ten pages there . . .

Suddenly, an image of Major Lhotsky had appeared before his mind's eye, but he wasn't sure whether this tall man in the uniform coat was not the major he had seen a few times in the Dolomite Alps—back when he had withdrawn to the Karersee with his *Everyman* draft—and whom he had considered incorporating in the play's dinner party. If something dated back a long time, it became more and more ghostly. Increasingly, memories of people he had met mingled with shadows that emerged in his own mind and claimed a life of their own.

He also remembered the thing that had suddenly started, deep in his insides, a queasy...

That year he had brought the baroness a signed copy of his dramatic poem *Yesterday*, and a few days later he had received a deckle-edge notecard with the family coat of arms on which she had thanked him in conventional phrases. (He remembered that the drama hadn't meant anything to good old Ferdinand von Saar either—at least Saar had written to him that the play was "no ordinary achievement.")

He had gone on a stroll with the letters in his overcoat pocket, mainly those his parents had forwarded from Vienna. Poldy Andrian had already departed for Switzerland with his family. Despite the presence of the Franckensteins and the Oppenheimers, Altaussee had suddenly felt deserted to him. He had taken the lake route, past the Andrian villa, and had opened the thick envelope on a bench to look through the letters. Stefan George had offered to make him one of the editors of *Blätter für die Kunst*. Next to the bench had sat a wooden garbage bin, where he had thrown some scrunched-up letters that no longer needed replies or which he did not intend to answer. He must have thoughtlessly thrown away the baroness's envelope and card, because a few days later, Georg Franckenstein told him on the tennis court that the Lhotskys were very disappointed in him. Somebody had found a letter the baroness had sent him in a garbage container on the path by the lake. "You had better not show your face at their house in the near future," Georg had said.

"But you have written such wonderful things about the festival, Herr von Hofmannsthal," the baroness had exclaimed. "About the primal theatrical drive of the Bavarian-Austrian people, about Salzburg's inimitable Baroque ensemble ... How beautifully you've expressed that, this reawakening of the Baroque festival. All this is in your head ... We simply must do something for our poor Austria. I also remember your patriotic articles in the *Neue Freie Presse* and in the *Rundschau* in those awful years. My husband read *The Affirmation of Austria* to me. The line about how great deeds and intellectual achievements emerge even in places where people do not think sufficiently ahead ... I know I'm only paraphrasing. And how a transformative strength emanates from our army ... "

*Think ahead* ... It was a sentence from Goethe, he had explained to the baroness—if I remember correctly, from Eckermann's conversations with Goethe.

"What are your thoughts on the peace treaty?" the baroness had asked. "It's already been two weeks! Nothing else was to be expected, was there? On his last furlough, my dear Laszlo, rest his soul, said that perhaps we should have been more accommodating to the Serbs in the summer of fourteen . . . We wouldn't necessarily have lost face by doing so, he said. You know that the major fell in the Carpathian Mountains a year and a half ago? At least he did not have to witness the unfortunate outcome of this war and our bank's bankruptcy."

He had thought about the newspaper report that the accommodations of the Austrian delegation in Saint-Germain, of which his friend Georg von Franckenstein was a member, had been fenced with barbed wire and manned by armed guards.

"By the way," the baroness had added, "the major read almost everything you published, and he always wondered why you omitted the military world from your writings, unlike Schnitzler, for example. Surely, you have nothing against our lieutenants?"

He remembered how he had opened the newspaper with the report and the drawing of the assassination in Sarajevo that wretched summer—Gerty had begun packing the bags for Altaussee—and, although everybody in Vienna had already heard about it, had suddenly felt a piercing stab in his chest. Everyone he knew, everyone except Schnitzler, had been in agreement that this time they could not let what the Serbs had done pass. Could anyone have prevented the House of Austria from falling apart? Might Prince Eugene have prevented it?

"Then I'll become Swiss," he had replied to the baroness's question as to what he thought of Austria possibly merging with Germany. "Although—" he had added, "although

I do have my readers, my audience, abroad; after all, the Burgtheater doesn't perform my plays."

Somewhere in the house, a telephone had rung as he had been getting ready to say goodbye. The baroness had left the room. "Vinzenz, why the deuce do you not answer the telephone?"

Vinzenz? he had thought. If the baroness sees my comedy, she will probably think that I have taken her servant from her. People always thought that they must mention to him—at times with indignation, at times flattered—that they recognized themselves in the character of Ariadne or that of Ochs. He had not finished writing this Vinzenz, however. In Ferleiten, he had made some notes for a new comedy with a rebellious servant in the leading role.

And he remembered that he had considered incorporating the baroness into the *Great World Theater*, in the role of the World.

When he was at last in visual proximity to the bench oriented toward the valley, he saw two mountaineers strapped with ropes and pickaxes approaching on the steep path leading up from the village. Thank God they only passed by the bench and issued a friendly greeting when he encountered them. Had they been exploring the Glockner area?

He wiped down the bench's slats with the used handkerchief from his hip pocket. A young man pushed a bicycle past him, and H. wondered where one would ride it here. Perhaps up on the level ridgeway, his favorite walkway in Fusch this time around. He remembered that he had brought his bicycle to Fusch one summer, in eighteen hundred and ninety-seven. Not to ride it up here but to meet Schnitzler and Beer-Hofmann in Zell am See and cycle to Salzburg with them. It was the summer that he had ridden his bicycle from Zell am See to Italy, via South Tyrol and Verona to Varese. I could, he thought, write something about that someday, just for myself. Those weeks in Varese had without doubt been the most productive in his entire life. He had written *The Small World Theater* during that time, *The Woman at the Window*, *The White Fan*, *The Emperor and the Witch*, and several other things.

A young man was approaching from afar, from the direction of the village. Was Doctor Krakauer avoiding his company now? He would regret that very much. Eighteen hundred and ninety-six, he thought, my God, what a beautiful late summer and autumn that had been, the year of my graduation. To feel oneself suddenly emerge from one's inner cocoon and really perceive the world. And then—what Stefan George called "currying favor with the masses"—the ever more frequent drafts for dramas and adaptations accumulating in his notebooks.

That evening, he remembered, he had strolled by the vacant Andrian villa in Altaussee; it had been his first time in Aussee without his parents. The Andrians had long departed, but through an open window he had noticed, as he had been approaching, a man singing while pacing back and forth, who had then sat down—he could see this through the row of windows—at the piano in the adjacent room and had continued to sing; it had sounded like Brahms. He had been introduced to him some days later in a restaurant's outdoor garden in the circle of his remaining friends: Raoul Richter, about his age, from northern Germany, related to the Andrians, invited to come stay for a few weeks after a serious illness. Because he had liked the look on Richter, he had proceeded to also try shaving only every three or four days. (He looked like a coachman, Felix Oppenheim had commented.) They had gradually become friends. Richter was the first of his northern friends.

That evening was unforgettable when Richter guided him into the woods in the dark and showed him a giant solitary fir and declared that it was his last day, that he would depart the next morning.

Years later he had tried, unsuccessfully, to find the way to this fir again. Instead, he had discovered, hiking from Altaussee via Obertressen to Bad Aussee one day, a bench underneath a linden tree, sat down, and immediately realized: a place to work! And when they—by now a family of five—had rented that farmhouse in Obertressen, he had found this very bench again on his first exploratory stroll; the farmer had set up a small table for him in front of it. It had been there that he had worked on his *Florindo* and the first drafts of *The Difficult Man*. Ever since once having found the bench occupied by an elderly Viennese couple in hiking clothes unwrapping bread, bacon, and pickled gherkins, he always had the same thought whenever it was empty:

This makes my day! Enjoying the view, the landscape, was a feat he had been managing ever more infrequently. He had started feeling unwell as Jakob Wassermann had pointed out the "fantastic mountain panorama" on the Loser Peak. The contours seemed to blur ever more often.

Since this wretched war had started, he had not visited that rough-slatted bench. When Eberhard von Bodenhausen had written to him in the second year of the war, *I imagine you in Aussee sitting at that small table in the woods . . .* he had felt almost hurt and responded, *I have not seen this spot again, have not stepped foot in this forest again. I cannot do it. My heart is too attached to all these things, so I do not want to go back, with a heart constricted, a soul in tight fetters, to this place that allowed me to ascend and descend into the bliss of eternity . . . I have been so fortunate to have had this—but it is awfully hard to have to do without it in the midst of life. For just as this little forest, as the world itself, my inner world, too, is before me: as an inaccessible . . .*

This summer is not lost after all, he had thought that difficult year of nineteen hundred and nineteen. The fairy tale finished, the prose version of *The Woman Without a Shadow*, maybe his best work. After a months-long illness, the three weeks of July in the Fusch valley, where he had not read so much as a newspaper, had restored him. *The Difficult Man* was as good as completed, a big folder with notes about the novel's sequel, some new comedies outlined and drafted. The comedies allowed him to take seriously people with their weaknesses, their absurdities. The negotiations in Salzburg had been felicitous, and the actor Alexander Moissi had finally committed to playing *Everyman* on the cathedral square the following summer.

He abruptly turned around. There was nobody to be seen on the path behind him, or up on the tiny flat square in front of the small church that sat slightly elevated at the edge of the forest. Nobody was currently sitting on any of the benches facing the church, in the small square, the so-called park in between the chestnut trees planted in a circle there countless years ago. Now he was looking forward to a cup of tea. Since the concierge had told him in a whisper two days ago that a young man, probably German, had asked for Herr von Hofmannsthal, he had at times been on the verge of sensing ghosts . . .

"But I remembered," Herr Widmayer had said, "what you had requested of me when you arrived."

He had thanked the concierge, and it became clear to him once again that because of the exorbitant amounts in which banknotes were denominated nowadays, one automatically hesitated when it came to tipping. He had wished for an undisturbed stay in Fusch, and—so far, at least—his wish had been fulfilled; at the same time, he had the impression that he had never before been so alone anywhere in the world.

It was almost like in his childhood years, when he had felt so dreadfully lonely in Fusch. His parents had had their acquaintances. Like his parents, many spa guests from Graz or Vienna—even from New York, Manchester, or

Düsseldorf—had been coming every year, but he was bored with those old ladies and gentlemen who swapped their top hats for Tyrolean headgear and resigned themselves incredibly to the meager level of comfort. Added to that was the frequent rainfall, so that he often could not even go for walks or read one of the books he had brought along in some corner of the hotel terrace.

Only years later, when he had started writing poems and met the Viennese writer Gustav Schwarzkopf, had his stays in Fusch become more bearable; still he always longed for the subsequent weeks in Strobl am Wolfgangsee, where he could swim, go sailing, play tennis, where he had met his closest friend, Edgar Karg von Bebenburg, and got together with him time and again, usually for short periods: A naval cadet in the Imperial and Royal Navy never received more than two weeks off. And in any case, his mother had been entitled to spend time with him first, as had his girlfriend, Lisl Nicolics, and his sister. Since he had found the note from his wife in the mail yesterday, in which she informed him that Christiane had kept in correspondence with Rudolf Borchardt, that someone from Borchardt's circle wanted to arbitrate their dispute, to reconcile them, and had inquired about his specific whereabouts, the idea had annoyed him that somebody might indeed come up to Fusch and importune him with this bothersome matter. If anything, of this he was convinced, only time could bring the affair with Borchardt back into balance. An intervention would only make matters worse; that had also been

Carl's opinion. Rudolf—it had been immediately clear to him at the time—had simply not found the words to write about him or his creation. Who knew better than he how hard it was to write something for a magazine, for a specific occasion, without the time needed to explain the subject's work in depth? Gerty had been a repeated witness to his groaning, to his frequent expressions of regret that he had consented to doing something, and eventually, after painful efforts, something would come to fruition, although he did not know how. Indeed, too much had gone awry in that Festschrift for his fiftieth birthday. Borchardt apparently had dedicated to him a brilliant finished or half-finished autobiographical excursion about his younger years, his upbringing, and his education in imperial Germany's foundational period, and had lectured readers in an uninspiring manner about the honoree's juvenilia. "So everything I have done since is nothing?" he had said to Gerty as she had tried to comfort him. "Won't you look at all the flowers," she exclaimed, "this sea of flowers in the parlor—is *that* nothing?"

I had just turned around to find you, dear Doctor Krakauer. The other day you actually followed me in person, when I felt your presence behind me up there by the church. This time, apparently, the wish was father to the thought, as the saying goes . . . Ever since you told me that Baroness Trattnig was jealous of me—I cannot judge how serious she was—I have feared that you are spending too much time reading that volume of my collected works or talking to me. At the same time, since we did speak about the baroness's volatility, I would have deeply regretted it if you had suddenly left Bad Fusch. The thought of perhaps having you as our guest in Rodaun during the winter months lifts my spirits. You might have noticed—I forgot to mention it to you the other day—that I included only the last part of *The Letters of the Man Who Returned* in this new edition. I remember that in the *Prose Writings*, published in nineteen hundred and seventeen, I also included only letters four and five. Myself, I have long been reluctant to identify with the beginning. The first chapter especially seems a partial failure to me, the conceptual outweighing the rest, the translation into prose, into sensuous representation, lacking...

One time, he remembered, he had pondered whether he had in fact conceded the point to Stefan George when discussing the danger of slipping into the world of the litterateurs, into newspaper writing. After all, *The Man Who Returned*, the first two parts, had first been published in the *Berliner Morgen*. The lack of approval from some of his friends had led him to lower his own estimation of these letters—until he had had that conversation with Pannwitz, who apparently had been very impressed with this work.

Now he thought, I'm already imagining letters to Doctor Krakauer! Well, why not?

Last night, while I was lying awake after a terrible dream, something happened. I would like to talk to you about it if you could make yourself available for an hour some time without flustering the baroness too much. It's possible that your confession yesterday in the quarter hour we met at the resort had a strong effect on me: You considered parting with the baroness, who you thought might be too possessive in the long run, and perhaps returning to the Vienna General Hospital.

Likewise your commitment to Elisabeth, whom I met only once on the hotel's terrace and of whom I didn't and don't know what her relationship to you might be. I was very moved when you told me that you had known Elisabeth for one and a half years, since you had entered the services of the baroness, but ever since you had heard her sing Hugo Wolf at the *Kammeroper* in Vienna in the last concert of the season a few weeks ago, you said you'd been fostering deep feelings for her. So you fell in love with her singing voice first. How beautiful, how well I can imagine that! The other day, you only told me that Elisabeth and her parents had sunk into abject poverty since the war, that she served as the baroness's companion, insofar as her artistic work allowed it. That the baroness would promote Elisabeth's career. (Now I know whose voice I have sometimes heard coming from one of the third-story windows in recent days. I take it she was practicing the arias from *La Traviata*.)

*I just read your message, Herr Doktor, the one you slipped under my door—probably during the night or in the morning, visibly written in a hurry. Now I almost regret that I gave you the volume of my new collected works and that you've spent too much* time reading my old things. That you—this is my feeling—have been neglecting the baroness because of it.

It is past ten o'clock, I'm sitting in the reading room reading your lines again. Surely you are—as you are informing me—well on your way by now to Zell am See, continuing on to Salzburg, with the baroness and Elisabeth. So I take it you will not read my note, which I will leave with the concierge, until tomorrow evening. Here it has started to drizzle; the prolonged stroll that I had been looking forward to since before I got up, to get clarity on some things while on foot, probably won't happen today.

Too much already, forgive me.


*Evening*

The concierge told me you wouldn't be back until Sunday. I have loved Salzburg since my childhood, had imagined before my departure from Switzerland that if I made good headway with my work in Fusch I could go to this charming town for two days, to treat myself, to sit on the terrace of the Café Tomaselli and look out over the Old Marketplace. Much has changed there, too, since the war, but they still have two waiters who were already there previously, whom I don't have to tell which coffee, which newspaper I like—even if I haven't been there in years. Now with the postal bus, the journey is no longer as time-consuming as it used to be. But you—or the baroness?—have your own automobile. Should my financial situation improve in the next years, we might also acquire such a useful vehicle. Having one has many advantages, as I recently learned in Graubünden.

*When I imagine the ordeals people—my parents included—incurred around nineteen hundred to get from Vienna to Bruck and on to Bad Fusch—that alone is a day's journey—and added to that going uphill with the horse carriage on that agonizingly narrow road! Sometimes we were so exhausted when we arrived that we collapsed into our beds without dinner . . .*

*On the way from Buchs to Zell am See I had resolved not to write any letters in Bad Fusch, to focus entirely on my work, on the play. But everything turned out differently. I often scare myself, how reclusive I have become. And when, conversely, nobody knows me here anymore, and nobody asks for me, that sometimes annoys me as well. I have no choice but to concede to myself that this war has accelerated the decline of our brittle culture to a degree that I could never have imagined. And it is hard for me to admit that I, too, originally thought going to war was the right thing to do. Like most people, however, I didn't know the reasons behind it, the endless stupidity with which a few people in Vienna and in Berlin spurred events in the summer of nineteen hundred and fourteen. Like many others, I wished for a real bloodbath for once. That might set things straight, I imagined . . .*

*When on my second day in Bad Fusch the concierge told me in a whisper that a young gentleman from Germany had asked for me, I feared that the circle around Rudolf Borchardt might have sent someone to achieve a reconciliation. You must know that a Festschrift was produced at the beginning of the year, on the occasion of my fiftieth birthday, which included, among others, contributions by some of my closest friends. It was all* well-intentioned, yet I was so aggravated when I began reading the texts to the extent that I had to lie down in my bed. My friendship with Borchardt may well be over.

Then again, I imagined that Rudolf Pannwitz had sent a delegate—as he had done before; he is an author whose writings, especially his Crisis of European Culture, I had greatly admired during the difficult final war years . . . Years ago, this man sent letters to my house almost daily, letters sometimes spanning ten pages or more. Reading those letters alone cost me much too much time. Moreover, the man turned out to be a brazen, at times half-insane man, so that I—after having collected money on his behalf in Vienna for years—gradually had to break off correspondence with him. Brecht, finally, that university professor to whom I recommended the climatotherapeutic spa town of Bad Fusch when he asked me about a summer retreat, of course before I had the idea in Switzerland to travel here myself. I sometimes enjoy conversing with him, he possesses a wealth of literary knowledge, but I wouldn't want him here now. He and his endearing but talkative wife would distract me too much.

Too much of all that already, dear Herr Krakauer: I actually just wanted to explain to you how much people dismay me at the moment, especially when they want something from me—and thus explain my unforgivable behavior toward the baroness. But it is indeed inexcusable.

There are moments in life, Herr Doktor, that are like milestones, instants in which it becomes clear to us that nothing will ever be the same as before. One knows that life will be divided

*into two parts from now: the time before and the time after. I*
*hope that we can talk about this soon. It is as if one suddenly*
*steps over a threshold into a still ghostly space, and then there's*
*only the final threshold left to cross . . .*

He should finally write to Josef Redlich, apologize for having been unable to visit him—from Lenzerheide, as they
had arranged—in his nearby holiday residence of Vulpera.
He asked the waiter for another cup of coffee and looked
up from the letter Paul Zifferer had written to him. In
it, Zifferer suggested, among other things, taking a trip
to Morocco together next spring. More and more guests
stepped out onto the terrace, but Krakauer and his baroness
were not among them.

He also had to reply to dear Max Rychner: What, he
had pondered several times in the past two weeks, could I
give him for his *Schweizer Rundschau*? In Lenzerheide he had
hoped to have a piece of his *Timon* ready enough to offer
to someone.

A smell of hay wafted by. Suddenly a strong yearning
pierced his breast, for his study at home, the couch behind
his desk, the garden, the gazebo in which so much had been
conceived in his younger years. What a shame that the climate at home so afflicted his head. How simple everything
would be! Why even have that beautiful garden with all the
flowers blooming in summer, in which he had hardly been
able to take pleasure for so many years?

When he had read the letters of young Goethe in his

garden over three afternoons, during his first summer in Rodaun, in order to write something about it, a fictional letter, first to his friend Karg von Bebenburg and then for a new edition from the Cotta publishing house. Such happiness: These youthful letters from a warm, often glowing sensibility, these were works of literature, "so beautiful one could cry," as Max Reinhardt always used to say. He regretted not having the volume of Goethe's letters in his luggage. What luck, back then, the connection of these letters with his dearest friend, whom he wanted to encourage to read—who knows on which warship and upon which seas he might be right now; there hadn't been any letters from him in a long time. And the summery garden. There is, he had thought at the time, no better place in the world to read these letters. And he had read some of the letters to Gerty when she passed by with a watering can in her hands.

The afterword to *Indian Summer*, which he had until late autumn to submit. He reached for the notes on the table. In the morning, when he had been looking through the papers for *The Tower*, he had come across three sheets on which he had jotted a few ideas about Adalbert Stifter in Lenzerheide:

*Passion and rapt enthusiasm the primal source, as in Jean Paul. (Passion remains in the subject, instead of entering the figures as in Balzac.)*

*Fear of passion, so that it cannot cloud the self's mirror to the world...*

*Created ideal images by way of elimination: omitting the viper in Stifter . . .*

It was then that he remembered the viper that had played dead on the forest trail a few days ago. When he stopped to see what it would do, it finally snaked its way, conspicuously slowly—as if it wanted to make it plain that this was no flight reaction—into the underbrush. And how it had hissed!

He began writing the clean copy of the corrected dialogue.

*A city in Asia Minor during the fall of Greece. People are facing political upheaval, and the much talked-about Timon is the radical leader of the petty bourgeoisie. The interlocutors are: Bacchis, a mime; Agathon, a poet; Kratinos, a philosopher; and three noblemen: Palamedes, Periander, and Demetrius . . . as well as Phanias, an impoverished great gentleman.*

Phanias: *You will experience many things. Timon will turn things upside-down for you. He is what will be, and it shall be my pleasure.*

Demetrius: *You think him a great man?*

Phanias: *I take him for an impertinent bastard dog. But the mouth on him is such that all the idle working riffraff gathers around him.*

Agathon: *The power of the demos is a mystery.*

Bacchis: *And what do you think of the power of the demos, my teacher?*

Kratinos: *My thoughts are slow. Like the sea they first cleanse each thing of its self-decay. I think the power of the demos is an illusion. It is one of the disguises of nothingness; like the future, progress, and the self.*

Agathon: *Demos harbors the tyrant within; one must merely give it time to bring him forth.*

"Would you like to join me at my table, Herr Krakauer? Today, it won't be possible to take breakfast on the veranda . . . First I must offer a belated apology for the other day. I haven't seen you and the two ladies since then . . . You know, I sometimes find my own unsociability quite uncanny, but what can I do? My wife often berates me for it. I sent you a letter, no, two letters—but one merely in my thoughts, while I strolled to the Fürstenquelle. I am especially sorry that I have hurt Baroness Trattnig; I don't know what was the matter with me. After all, she simply asked me why there will be no festival this year. What would I have lost if I had explained to her that the reasons given in the newspaper articles—a female lead having quit, shortage of money—were untrue?"

Krakauer massaged his face and eyes with both his hands, as if he wanted to free himself from something or other.

"The main reason," H. continued, "was more the catastrophic situation in the whole country. Inflation, a shortage of housing, and unemployment are a huge burden on the locals, and it is very difficult in such times to find support for the festival. A certain reactionary outlet by the telling name of *Der eiserne Besen*, The Iron Broom, keeps stirring up animosity against festival director Max Reinhardt. In any case, there was concern that festively dressed visitors arriving from all over Europe and even overseas would be harassed by the locals in front of the festival hall. I would have felt terrible if you and the baroness had unknowingly traveled to the city for a festival event. I will, of course, make a formal apology to the baroness in person at the next opportunity. Perhaps the opportunity will arise in the course of the day..."

"No, no," said Krakauer, "she should not have ambushed you like that on the staircase. But that is how she is. Then again, she can be quite...ill-tempered herself. She is not well. As strong as a horse physically, but mentally quite unstable. Well, the resort's physician has prescribed some healing baths and extended hikes. I have little to contribute myself. But she seems to set great store by my company. Someday I would like you to meet her niece, Elisabeth, whom I have mentioned to you before, if I remember correctly. She is still quite unknown as a singer. For many years now, the baroness has been something of a second mother to her, even if she treats her quite rudely at times, as I have witnessed myself. Elisabeth was offered an engagement at the Budapest opera house, but the baroness became terribly agitated when she heard about it—that was before I became associated with the two ... I am their private physician, so to speak. Well, she can afford it ... I read a lot; the baroness does, too, by the way. She loves Rilke, *serafico*, as the Princess of Thurn and Taxis calls him. Elisabeth, however, cannot be bothered to take a walk, though it would be very important for her as well. She does not have the right footwear and warm attire. We almost *fled* Salzburg—all of a sudden, the baroness wanted to leave the city. And that's why either today or tomorrow we will go back to Zell am See once again to get Elisabeth the proper equipment.

"In her room in the half-empty Hotel Post she was able to practice her scales. But nothing satisfied the baroness there, she even found the silverware and napkins abominable. Now with the Grand Hotel almost at capacity, singing is no longer possible... At the beginning of October, Elisabeth will make her appearance as Countess Maritza, rehearsals were set to start in five weeks. In any case, the baroness cannot bear to be anywhere very long; I've already insinuated as much. When the weather worsened yesterday, it presented a setback to us in terms of walking. The resort's physician, Doctor Schieferer, told me that the mortality rate in this area was one of the lowest in the entire monarchy. Used to be. Above all, it's the tranquility here—the clean, crisp air and the intense sunlight to boot—that is supposed to be salutary for the psyche. We've already chosen a new hiking trail: to the Hirzbach waterfall. There, in that area, they are said to have dug for gold... The area does not appear on my map, however."

H. replied that he did not have his old travel guide for Bad Fusch and the surrounding area on him, since he had not planned to go into Fusch initially. But the concierge would surely be of help. He could not remember ever having visited the Hirzbach waterfall, but he had been to the Kesselbach falls several times. He highly recommended a hike to Weixelbachhöhe, which he had done every year in earlier days. If one continued to hike from there a good bit farther, one would get an open view of the Seidlwinkl valley. He had never made it all the way to Rauris, however, as it would have required staying overnight.

Actually, said Krakauer looking at his watch, he was supposed to fetch a pot of tea for the baroness, who did not want to leave her room. Later, he himself would . . . You couldn't leave the baroness alone at present.

"You look pale, Herr von Hofmannsthal. I would like to take your blood pressure. May I trouble you to see me in my room later?"

In the mornings, he replied, he would often feel more spent than in the evenings before going to sleep. It was only after drinking coffee that he would come alive.

"I don't care for the tea here anymore; perhaps it's me, I don't know. Switzerland has spoiled me, I suppose . . . "

"Switzerland wasn't stupid enough to start a war," said Krakauer.

H. felt an aversion rise inside him. Yet the doctor was certainly right. And ever since he had read Austrian general Conrad von Hötzendorf's memoirs, the first volumes of which had been published recently, and those of a French diplomat, he understood with horror that the fault for the war's outbreak lay entirely with the Austrians and the Germans, all the terrible idiocies, the mad delusions of grandeur, ignorance in the face of the political situation . . . A few people in Vienna and in Berlin were to blame for the deaths of millions.

"You are absolutely right. It is as if monstrosities some-how yearned to break out, no matter how...Years ago, I already felt very bad things were to come, inevitably...the southern Slavs in the monarchy, not only the Serbs, also the Croats...turmoil, summary executions...the Bohemians lurking with their teeth bared, Galicia infiltrated by Russian agitators, Italy just as comfortable being an enemy as it is an ally, Russia thirsting for an attack...And a kind of panic brewing at the center of the monarchy...Everyone should have sensed that we were steering toward dark times. In all this I had to think of my children first and foremost...I apologize, don't let me keep you. Please relate my regret about my awful thoughtlessness to Baroness Trattnig; it's my nerves...

"You know, it is like a neurotic obsession for me to shun people here; each new face spooks me...Anyway, I can't stand most faces anymore. It is a completely different society from that of before the war...The aftermath will keep us busy for many years to come. A good friend of the family, Sebastian Isepp—yes, Sebastian, like you—a very good painter, he had to witness several battles at the Isonzo Front, was twice buried by rubble. He survived but stopped painting in light of everything he had endured during those terrible years. Since the war's end he has devoted all his time to restoring artworks...In some ways, the rubble has also buried me, in the last years of the war. Inside me... things are buried inside me, and I no longer have access to them."

"I am very eager to see the *The Difficult Man* in the theater...I don't even know: Have you written comedies before?"

"The poet Novalis said somewhere that you must write comedies after an infelicitous war," he replied, "no, wait, he said, the portrayal of things past is a tragedy and all portrayals of things to come, a comedy...No, I'd have to reread that passage. I don't have my Novalis edition with me. Well, I don't know whether there has ever been a *felicitous* war; even though some of them may have been necessary. Yes, well, I've written a few comedies, most recently, *The Incorruptible*. Nothing worth mentioning, really, a conversational play that I did as an afterthought of sorts, but Viennese audiences liked it last year.

"Well, I will go for a walk now," he said while Krakauer pulled out his pocket watch once again. "At least the rain seems to have stopped. I hope to be successful in settling in here. With my work, I mean, of course. When I am in my room, move my table to the window, sit with my papers, look out at the Kreuzköpfl—whose outermost peak went white again yesterday, by the way—I am lost in thought, in the Fusch of yesteryear. If I then leave my room, climb down the stairs, and reach the foyer, I realize that everything has changed.

"I admit, my yearning for Aussee is enormous. If my wife hadn't dissuaded me from doing it, I would have departed long ago. But I know from experience that nothing would change if I did. Before mid-August, I'd have no peace in our little house there. The small room in the outbuilding, my study, is where my daughter sleeps. This should not bother me; after all, I work by day. But every foreign presence—and when I write, even my wife is foreign to me—irritates the imagination and my associative faculties... One minor disturbance, and I might lose an entire day. Reality keeps throwing its monkey wrench into the works of our imagination, doesn't it?"

Krakauer looked at his watch again and said he had spent the years after nineteen hundred and twelve with his uncle in New York, had started studying at Columbia University. Three years later, he actually had wanted to return to Vienna—but had decided to finish his studies in the United States after all.

"We simply must talk about your *Man Who Returned*—excuse me, Herr von Hofmannsthal, I *would* very much like to do so, because I... I initially had a very hard time getting used to seeing the city of Vienna so impoverished, and like your man who returned, I also felt that the people had changed tremendously."

A waiter appeared, served Krakauer a tray with a teapot and two cups. Initially, he had a very hard time getting used to seeing the city of Vienna so impoverished, Krakauer repeated.

Suddenly he felt able to write Harry Kessler the letter he had long wanted to write. How happy he had been when Count Kessler had broken their long silence last fall, had written such a touching letter, from out at sea. The immediate occasion, apparently, had been a visit to the tomb of Charles I in Funchal on the island of Madeira, where the hapless monarch had died two years prior.

*My dear friend . . . How much I miss, at present, a superior, gripping intellect like yours for helpful conversation . . . After having been able more or less to finish the revised version of* The Tower *in Switzerland, I am currently occupied with the political comedy Richard Strauss had encouraged me to write, set in Athens in the third century. I told you about it that time in Berlin. Those conversations with you during our joint work on the* Rosenkavalier *were a singular experience; only much later could I fully appreciate the significance of your ideas, your criticism . . .*

It had suddenly become clear to him why this long-standing, amicable relationship with Kessler could not have endured: His sensitive nerves had become less and less able to tolerate Kessler's heated, tense temperament. He also couldn't forget what Eberhard von Bodenhausen had once told him in confidence: Kessler held the view that he, H., had *absolutely no constructive talent to invent and to arrange a dramatic story line, which is why he relies on existing scenarios.* But if an effective scenario was available, Kessler opined, Hofmannsthal had the gift of animating it with wonderful lyricism, to breathe life into the characters and situations . . .

Oh, I'm so glad, he had thought, that Count Kessler accredits me with lyrical talent—while I myself am more and more afraid that I might lose my lyrical gift. Years ago, he had come across some words by Hegel with which he partly agreed. In essence, they purported that the lyrical poet was the exemplary embodiment of a young person intoxicated by the soaring flights of his soul. Adolescence, then, was a time in which a person, focused on himself, was unable to be clearly aware of his environment. And as soon as the artist crossed the threshold from immaturity to maturity, he would also leave the lyrical realm forever. He immediately thought of Valéry as an exception, who, at the same age as he, had recently published a comprehensive collection of poems entitled *Charmes*.

On the way back from the Fürstenquelle, he approached the car lot at the edge of the town where he had recently gone to view the stationary automobiles. There was no Maybach, like the one Carl owned, among them. H. enjoyed riding in automobiles. He—like his wife—liked to be chauffeured, but on the ride from Lenzerheide into the Val Bregaglia he was occasionally scared by the gorges, the precipices, so close to the edges of the winding roads; the many bends also repeatedly made him feel queasy, and they had to take breaks. A car with a chauffeur, he thought, my financial situation would have to improve a lot for that. He had spent most of his payment for the premiere of *Alcestis* in March on the Italian journey. He had placed high hopes on the motion picture adaptation of the *Rosenkavalier*, but negotiations were slow-moving. But he knew full well that the translation of the libretto into American English was impossible, that something completely different would be made of it in the end, and that he, sitting in the movie theater, would start crying with horror.

He didn't even recognize Doctor Krakauer at first, when he waved at him, travel bag in hand, wearing a leather cap and motoring goggles pushed up on his forehead. A lady, equally hooded and bespectacled, sat in the automobile with the top down. Krakauer got up, exited the vehicle, unbuttoned his brown leather coat. They had to go back down to fetch a few things for the baroness. They had spent the entire morning in the hospital, he said.

"Oh yes, you may not know yet—the baroness was found by two local boys in the woods yesterday noon, she had spent the night outdoors. She's already feeling better, physically . . . A terrible thing, we were looking for her everywhere around here yesterday.

"And earlier, there was almost a terrible accident at the Zell am See town limits. If I hadn't reacted in a flash there in front of the church, that Mercedes would have hit us much harder. The right front fender indented, the tire undamaged, thank God . . . "

To keep driving, he and the chauffeur of the Mercedes had to combine efforts to fix the dent in the thick fender.

Krakauer took off his cap and straightened his hair. He'd be happy if they were able to talk again, he said. He hadn't found the time to read in days. Yet he would love to really delve into *The Man Who Returned*. He had been able to get his hands on a volume of prose with the complete text in a bookshop on Residenzplatz in Salzburg. He would return the volume from the complete works to H. shortly.

He looked around.

"How shall I put it? It's absurd, but the baroness is jealous of you, Herr von Hofmannsthal. Only because twice I wasn't immediately available to her! I am so embarrassed. We were in Salzburg for two days—I may have already mentioned it: The baroness is a distant relation of the owner of Hotel Stein. An interesting man, he is the editor of a slender book about *Faust*. Well, the view from the hotel's roof terrace over the old part of town is indeed very impressive.

"We simply must talk about your *Letters of the Man Who Returned* . . . Excuse me . . . I hate to abuse your kindness. I am repeating myself, but I would really enjoy it.

"We took the funicular up to the fortress; we shared our compartment with an American couple, well, the wife was American, possibly very wealthy—we saw them again later, up at the restaurant. The husband was from Graz, no longer young, hadn't been back in Austria for twenty-five years . . . Excuse me!

"This is Elisabeth, I don't know if you've . . . Baroness Elisabeth von Trattnig, she will hopefully take the opera stages of the world by storm one day."

H. extended his hand to her. She seemed reserved. A light weatherproof cape of sorts, a loden skirt, a patterned silk neckerchief, cap, motoring goggles pushed up on her forehead.

"Her role model is the soprano Maria Jeritza," Krakauer added.

"Ah, how interesting," said H., "I've worked with Jeritza on several occasions. She sang my *Ariadne*, among others . . . "

"I know," said Elisabeth, who seemed to have awakened from her torpor.

"Well, aren't we all people who returned?" said H. and doffed his hat to bid goodbye. "I've just returned from a hike, will soon return to my Aussee, and in early November I will presumably return to Vienna, to Rodaun. When I arrived here, in the first two, three days, I felt like a man who returned everywhere, wherever I went—I first had to reacquaint myself with the place, the benches and wells and woods. Many things were strange to me at first, some have remained strange to me to this day . . . It's been so long. Many things have been newly built or rebuilt in the meantime . . . And you've just returned from Zell am See—no small feat, that drive up here, with the automobile, I imagine. Tomorrow I'd like to take the postal omnibus down, and in the afternoon I will return."

"I'm sure I will have to go back down later today," Krakauer called out as he turned around, "in case you want a ride."

"Not today," said H., "I must sit down at my desk, there's no way around it. I would gladly welcome any distraction . . . Oh, I forgot, I want to go to the post office to drop off a letter." And in so saying, he approached Krakauer again.

"I read your *Conversation between Balzac and Hammer-*

*Purgstall*," said Krakauer after fastening a strap in the back seat. "The story with the painter, Frenhofer, fascinates me, especially the part"—he looked around, lowered his voice—"where the young Poussin offers him his pretty young mistress as a model, as a sacrifice for art in a way, because Frenhofer had claimed that there were no more women with a perfectly beautiful body... Tell me, in which of Balzac's works would I find this Frenhofer story?"

H. put his hat back on.

"It should be in one of the volumes of his *Comédie Humaine*," he said. "I have a nice single-volume edition of it at home, in Rodaun. It is also an exploration of academic, neoclassicist and romantic painting. Yes, a wonderful artist novella. I don't even know anymore what influence it might have on my own work."

He thumbed through the second volume of his recently published collected works, which the concierge had delivered to him with Doctor Krakauer's calling card. He could not find *The Letters of the Man Who Returned* in the table of contents, then he remembered that he had adopted only two passages from these letters for this edition, under the title *The Colors*. The theme of perception was the central aspect of these fictional letters, the returned man's experience of color.

How the blazes had he come to write to Alma Mahler the previous night? He crumpled up the two pieces of paper that had been weighted down by the Henry James book, and also the note from Alfred Kubin, the hand-copied, almost illegible chain letter. That Kubin, what a lunatic. The nerve he had to make such a demand: *Copy nine times within twenty-four hours and forward to nine people of your choice.* Didn't the man have other things to do?

But Christiane's letter from Aussee had lifted his spirits. How in the world did she manage to do that every time? She wrote about reading Stendhal's *De l'Amour*. Now she finally understood the book. She had read it secretly at the age of twelve and couldn't make heads or tails of it. And Choderlos de Laclos's *Dangerous Liaisons*—that novel she stopped reading after a hundred and fifty pages ... about her friendship with Thankmar von Münchhausen ... And then there was Walther Tritsch ...

"Papa, why do men always try to break some barrier?" she once had asked him when telephoning home from Berlin. He hadn't had to worry about Christiane for some time now; her emotions and intellect had developed very nicely.

He reached for the open book of stories by James; one sentence he had marked: That travel was a "modern indignity, people's incessant loud chatter, their boorish, reckless behavior, their herdlike appearance ...

Dear Alma Mahler. Every once in a while, he remembered their meeting many years ago—Gustav Mahler had still been alive—in the foyer of the Vienna Court Opera; she had mentioned something to him concerning a ballet scenario of his, which Alexander von Zemlinsky still hadn't brought to the stage. She herself had ambitions of the compositional kind, he had thought, oh well ... And how she

had stood before him, almost goading him, sticking her voluminous breasts out at him, in a manner of speaking, an erotic
creature the likes of which he had seldom seen. In recent
years they had lost sight of each other.

His lower back was aching, he pushed it against the
backrest of his chair. Not one line written, only a few notes
that were promising. Spread out on the bed were sheets of the
manuscript for *The Tower*. At least the fifth act, which he had
resisted approaching for so long, he had been able to finish
in Lenzerheide. He was going to read it to Gerty in Aussee.

Since the war, it occurred to him, none of the Viennese
coffeehouses put out the *Prager Tagblatt* or *Czernowitzer
Morgenzeitung* for their guests anymore. In the restaurant,
the table candles flickered in art nouveau candelabras. Their
restless light fell on the faces of the married couple at the
neighboring table, which he found hard to stand. The man
wearing a dreadful imitation of an Emperor Franz Joseph
beard, the woman wearing a golden bonnet and a constric-
tor-like boa made of myriad small white feathers.

"Tonight, unfortunately, once again no electric light,"
the waiter had whispered to him at the entrance.

H. pondered telling him that it was drafty here, that he
should check if the door to the terrace was closed. On the
velour upholstery of the second chair at the table sat a portion
of the mail he hadn't wanted to open in his room and which
he would look through in the smoking lounge afterward,
over black coffee.

He had skimmed the letter from Ria Schmujlow-Claasen from the Bavarian Forest. His old friend was feeling ill. They were finally liquidating their apartment in Munich and planned to move to Rome. He last saw Ria this spring in Palermo. How her situation had moved him: Because her husband was a foreigner and a socialist, a wedding in Germany had not been approved at the time; they had had to get married in London. At the beginning of the war, Vladimir had then been deported from Germany. . . At present he felt unable to write a fitting reply to her letter and put it back in the envelope. Not a word from Ottonie from Bavaria for many weeks now.

For the next two days, the concierge had informed him, the barometer would stay low; but then, finally, Pinzgau was to expect midsummery weather for a longer period. That's no use to me anymore, he thought, I will leave in three, four days at the latest. He pushed the empty soup plate away. Last night, when he had lain awake for a long time, he had pondered having the concierge call for a coach from Bruck or Zell am See so he could simply depart after an early breakfast. He had dreamt of an avalanche in Fusch, of mountains of snow writhing along and burying everything. I, he had thought, have never witnessed a snowslide disaster, but the night before, he had thumbed through an old traveler's guide from the library and read about the terrible calamities of the past century. How often had these hotels been rebuilt from the ground up! And what should I do to get through two more days of bad weather? When my imagination is still failing me, even fueling my aversion to writing a single letter?

The Oppenheimer estate Ramgut in Altaussee came to his mind, with the study, the big library—how long had it been since he had worked there well into October? Good old Yella . . . He had written to her from Lenzerheide; he didn't know if and when she would come to Aussee with her family this summer. He had long drifted apart from Felix but in turn had become ever more familiar with his mother, with Yella, who had also become a mother of sorts to him. How many years had he had his room in the farm manor, in which he had also slept, working sometimes late into the night. The house's furniture darkened the rooms even more, so that on days of bad weather one had to light the desk lamp even by day. It was in that room that he had completed his *Florindo*. When had he first set foot in that house?

What was it like when my father was as old as I am now? He reckoned back, nineteen hundred and four . . . Everything drifted past him . . . How many years had he left to live? Nineteen hundred and fourteen . . . and now, nineteen hundred and twenty-four. All the things that had happened in between!

He left half of his schnitzel on the plate. "No dessert today," he said to the waiter. As soon as the waiter had cleared the table and smoothed out the tablecloth, H. reached for the mail and arranged it in front of him. First, he reread the short letter from his wife that she had enclosed. She once again reminded him that he might get a visitor in Fusch, a student from George's circles, an acquaintance of Rudolf Borchardt who wanted to mediate their dispute. She, at least, had told no one of his current whereabouts. An acquaintance of Borchardt? He did not want to imagine that this was Rudolf's doing. He had recently talked to Carl about this vexing issue. And once, in the morning, he had contemplated the way in which he might apologize to Borchardt without apologizing. After all, Borchardt was basically the only serious author and critic he felt understood him, as far as his work was concerned. But hadn't there been, from the very beginning, a delicate balance between attraction and repulsion?

He also considered apologizing to Carl for his rushed departure from Lenzerheide. He remembered that he had already wanted to leave on the first evening, because the young director of the Park Hotel had given him the willies. Though he had liked that establishment so much upon their arrival that he resolved to return next year.

Am I slowly going insane? he thought. What is my work on those plays doing to me? I couldn't even tell Carl the true reason for breaking off my stay! The day he apologized to Carl after breakfast for his bad mood on the drive to Davos. When they got there, he had been shocked by the many funeral parlors, the many coffin emporia. Before breakfast, while waiting for Carl, he had picked up a *Berner Zeitung*, had thumbed through it, until on one of the pages in the back he had come across three short prose poems by Robert Walser. And suddenly he had felt as if everything were collapsing on top of him.

Just leave, he had thought, again and again, I can't take it here anymore! Especially one sentence had remained unforgettable to this day: "When did I lose the fine dusting of the butterfly in me?" Shortly thereafter, Carl had appeared at breakfast, apologized for his tardiness, asked him how he was feeling this morning, and immediately H. had dropped his spoon.

The thought at that moment over the sheet of newspaper: Over! Finished! There's no point! Leave the play, that *Timon*, be, and just take a vacation, to the extent that it is possible. Sit here and drink coffee, here at the Park Hotel, drink tea, read newspapers, a book, go for walks, write a few letters, take a long nap; stay in the room in the afternoon when the heat is unbearable, or go to a bench in the woods to read...

The conversation with Carl had calmed him down somewhat, and he immediately agreed enthusiastically when Carl suggested driving to Soglio in the Val Bregaglia someday, very early in the morning.

At the circular junction he had to step aside to make way for a small, rocking automobile operated by a young lady.

When was that? he pondered. When that winter in Berlin had he happened upon Borchardt, who had been giving a lecture for Walther Rathenau in a villa on Wilhelmstrasse during a furlough from the front? Nineteen hundred and sixteen? Back then, while spending several weeks in Berlin working for the Foreign Ministry, he had finally had ample occasion to converse with Max Reinhardt, which had invigorated him immensely. Within a few days he had written some things in his room at the Adlon; a ballet after Molière's *The Imaginary Invalid*, an adaptation of a Raimund play, and the *Troublesome*—advertised as a play by Molière but written by him . . . And finally, another ballet, *The Green Flute*. He had also had all these things to organize for the performances for Reinhardt . . . adaptations, pantomimes . . . Suddenly he had become so immersed in his work that he even had had no trouble writing the adaptation of Molière's prelude to *Ariadne*, the new version to be performed at the Vienna Court Opera in October.

Singing could be heard from somewhere, from some window, a woman was practicing her scales—that must have been Elisabeth . . . He stopped, took off his hat, wiped the sweat from his brow. So at least they were still here. He hadn't seen Krakauer in the last two days. Now the famous aria from *La Traviata*. Why did it remind him of the frightful scene from *Otello*, of the evening on the Schönenberg in Carl's home, recently, a few days before they had left for Lenzerheide? Right in the middle he had asked Carl to pick up his gramophone's needle from the record and to replay Iago's aria *Credo in un Dio crudel che m'ha creato simile a sè* . . . He had wanted to find out what had frightened him so terribly, but upon the second listen, the fright did not recur. Carl had offered to ask his sister for the lyrics booklet, knowing that she had a copy in her music collection. Then they could read the entire passage from the second act.

He considered, if it ever came to a meeting, asking the

baroness whether she had read the article in today's *Salzburger Volksblatt* about the riding school of the Prince-Archbishopric of Salzburg, which was currently being renovated as a venue for the Salzburg Festival. That this renovation created many jobs appeased the resentment of certain circles in the populace. He had reached the bench by the church wall. Again, he thought of not opening the folder with his *Timon* for his remaining days here in Fusch. He liked to repeat to himself now and then that the war, that long interruption, was one of the reasons for his failure to work on the things he had planned to do, especially the novel.

Back then, many years ago, Ottonie had actually been very impressed when he had spent one hour reading to her from his novel fragment in Hinterhör one afternoon, about the adventures of Andreas Ferschengelder. She was often closer to him in his thoughts than almost anybody else had ever been; and when he saw her in Neubeuern, she sometimes seemed a stranger to him, and sometimes he had been glad to have been accompanied by Gerty, who noticed his torpor and lifted it with a few words. Of course, Ottonie had an inordinate amount of work to do, all those children she had looked after during the war years. But not only the children had found a place in Hinterhör, also disabled veterans, refugees, and she had to care for all of them.

In Aussee, he resolved, I will write to Rudolf Borchardt. What in the world has come over me? Also with Zifferer, to whom I owe so much, I probably would have bungled things, if he weren't such a loyal man. But I had to say something to him about his novel about the imperial city, silence would have offended him just as much. And I did decide long ago that I would give people who send me books my unadulterated opinion as soon as I have read them. Zifferer's novel, he thought, would almost lend itself to serialization in *Das Interessante Blatt*. Many writers, it seemed to him, were ready to fulfill the final wish of an era, once it already had been replaced by a new one . . .

A lady who moved past him to enter the church gave him a friendly nod. Now he remembered the word *espadrilles*, which he had been looking for the day before while sketching a scene for his *Timon*. This lady's white espadrilles, however, did not match her dirndl dress with the dark green apron at all. Ants scurried on the grouted stone slabs: Was this not a bad sign for the days to come? The first leaves had already fallen from the giant beech, perhaps due to the heavy winds the day before.

In earlier days, when he was young, he had been able to write poems in bad weather, when the barometer was low . . . He recalled Joseph Conrad, whose book of reminiscences, *A Personal Record*, he had read a few years ago. Never, he had thought at the time, never could I write a book about myself . . . In the small hotel library, where he had looked around the other day, there was a copy of *The Secret Agent*. Already in his youth, he had had the impression that this library was mainly or even exclusively composed of books—read or unread—left behind by guests. He himself, he remembered, had left books there that he had brought from Vienna and no longer had any intention of reading. He had even deposited extra copies of his own books there. A few days ago, he had discovered a small English-language volume that he was sure had belonged to him many years ago: *The Strange Case of Dr. Jekyll and Mr. Hyde and Other Stories*. Had he inadvertently left it there, or had he wanted to donate it to the library? He also spotted Ferdinand von Saar's elegies, the pretty little paperback with the red binding. No name was inscribed. No, he certainly had not left the Stevenson on purpose.

He took the little book in his hands and felt like reading the story again. Now he remembered when he had learned of Robert Louis Stevenson's passing in a newspaper in Fusch; his father had handed the newspaper to him in the reading room. Strange that the great authors always seemed to die in the summer months. A violent jolt went through him: Had he so repressed the news he had recently received that Walter Benjamin had fallen ill with cancer that he hadn't thought about it at all in the past few days? Nor about Benjamin's wonderful essay about Goethe's *Elective Affinities*, which he wanted to publish in his journal *Beiträge* as soon as possible? How he had looked forward to a meeting with the young author, whom Florens Christian Rang had recommended to him ... How careless: The news of the severe illness did not pertain to Benjamin but to Rang, which of course had made it no less shocking.

How the Weixel stream thundered down from on high, frothing, in overlapping, bubbling thrusts! How often had he stood on this bridge, in this at times mysterious spot, shaded on the right-hand side by sprawling, tall brickwork, the back of the Grand Hotel, on the left by the steep embankment, densely crowded with tall spruces—hard to believe that they could strike root here. Underneath the bridge on which he was standing, the torrents roared their way down the mountain, running into the valley below and into the Fuscher Ache, which flowed into the Salzach river near Bruck, the Salzach then flowing into the Inn, the Inn into the Danube, and finally the Danube into the Black Sea.

This is how I, he remembered, stood on a slightly larger bridge with Carl, in Lenzerheide; the broad stream there, however, seemed infinitely peaceful, its surface as smooth as a mirror, almost motionless, and they had talked about the work of Oswald Spengler again, and he had said that he had found himself unable to agree with Spengler's theories when he had read *The Decline of the West* for the first time, during the war, that he could not accept his severity and fatalism. Individual elements, however, he had added, had managed to convince him; he had incorporated a few things into his notes for *Timon*. Now, seven, eight years later, it sometimes seemed to him when he looked around, when he read the newspapers, that Spengler might have been right after all, that ours was a late period, a soulless, artless age governed by money and in which everything was determined by money. Sometimes, he had told Carl, he wondered if he wouldn't have long given up on his *Timon* had he not read Spengler's work. "It seems to me," he had

added, "that Spengler confirms my worldview, my observa-
tions; in some aspects we are in agreement, and this makes
my mind soar."

"Your blood pressure is definitely too high," Krakauer said.
"May I ask how many cups of coffee you imbibe every day?"
He placed the device on the bed, looked at the nightstand
with several books sitting atop.

H. shook his head.

"For years now I've felt like a disabled person. My nerves
have grown old faster than my body, an inheritance from my
mother . . . I shall need another go . . . This phrase, *another go*,
which keeps ambling around my head, is something my son
Raimund brought home from England. He tried to use it to
cheer up his older brother, Franz, who recently has not been
doing well at all abroad. It's actually from Henry James. You
might have come across this author in New York."

"But you are not old," Krakauer called out, "and I will
take care of you once we're back in Vienna come November.
I will have more time then, clear my schedule a little bit.
You know, my baroness is incredibly sensitive; she has low
self-esteem. You wouldn't expect it just by looking at her; she
can be quite callous sometimes, quite imperious . . . Her cat
ran away before our departure from Vienna, and she's had a
hard time getting over it. She almost canceled the reservation
for Bad Fusch. Sometimes Elisabeth, her niece, is terribly
vexed by her behavior . . . The coming days in Ischl will do
her good. We will drive the automobile down to Zell am See

after our meal. The baroness wants to buy some things, warm clothes. It is hard to believe: It seems as if spending the night outdoors has agreed with the baroness ... In principle, we're staying at least another week, the rooms are reserved until the twelfth of August. Well, unfortunately, so far her resort treatment has not had the effect I had hoped for. I want to browse the pharmacy in Zell am See. Also to see if I find something suitable for you. If you need anything from Zell am See, please do tell me.

"I would love to have more time to read. I spent much time last night reading your volume of prose, the *Conversation Between Balzac and Hammer-Purgstall*, for the second time. *Conversation in a Garden in Döbling* is the subtitle ... It stirs up a lot in me. Because I grew up in Döbling ... Despite being very tired, I was swept away by the dialogue. I will reread it many times to take it all in. As I will *The Letters of the Man Who Returned*. There are some philosophical passages in it, which I will probably grasp only upon a second reading. How could you have known what moved me during my journey home on the ship to Southampton? And especially in Vienna in those first months. Although you wrote about the conditions in Germany—but the differences are probably not so big. Your man was gone eighteen years before returning; that's a long time. I only spent eight years in the United States, and that already seemed long enough for me."

H. replied that when the text had been published in a newspaper, he sensed puzzlement, even hurt feelings, especially among some of his German friends. Some, to whom he had forwarded the newspaper excerpt, kept silent altogether. Many people couldn't make heads or tails of his *Balzac* either, by the way. He had regretted that. Made-up conversations and letters were really one of his favorite genres. There were grand masters in this field, Walter Pater, Fontanelle, Walter Savage Landor, Wieland . . . And not to forget Paul Valéry among the more recent authors . . . At the time, after the publication of his fictional Lord Chandos letter, he would have liked to have worked in this genre exclusively going forward, there were dozens of drafts, sketched-out ideas. But suddenly, he had had a family, children, and an obligation to earn money. So he had turned to theater and, after meeting in Berlin in nineteen hundred and six with Richard Strauss, who had wanted a libretto from him, had tried his luck there.

"In essence, I have written everything for my father, my first and best reader, as I've always thought. And then, after his death nine years ago . . . Had I not had a family to feed, who knows what I would have done. Sebastian Isepp, he always comes to mind. I have sometimes imagined putting my literary work on hold, at least for a few years. On the other hand, what would I have started doing, I cannot do anything else."

He pulled on his coat.

"It was here in Fusch," he continued, "that I told my father on a stroll that I could not imagine an academic career. By the way, there was some contact with the Ministry of Education through Hermann Bahr for a post as a cultural educator. Through this I got to know the bureaucracy in our administrative offices; it wouldn't have been an option for me anyway. After my marriage, I withdrew my petition to give some lectures at the university. We moved to Rodaun, the transportation network around the turn of the century was still inadequate. At the time, I was toiling away on a drama about Guido of Arezzo and his wife, Pompilia—a crime story of sorts. At last I seemed to have found the right material for a great drama. But what am I babbling on about, I am keeping you for no reason, please forgive me."

Krakauer softened his voice: He had made a decision last night, two decisions actually, regarding his future and that of Elisabeth. There was, he said, some bond between him and Elisabeth, maybe it was just a thin thread at this point, but it could be so much more. He had come to realize this on a stroll they had taken together recently in Salzburg, at the crack of day, when he had been standing next to her on the Mönchsberg looking out over the city.

"Elisabeth is afraid the baroness might turn away from her. The baroness doesn't like it when we part company with her, sit together, and talk. What she assumes or suspects is not true. Until now, at least. Today I told myself, this person is a true treasure . . . I would be delighted if you were able to get to know her a bit one of these days. Your *Man Who Returned* has led me to a decision that has been going around my head for a good while. To return to my own life . . ."

"While you were in Salzburg," H. said, "I wrote you a long letter. But as I'm trying to remember precisely what I wrote, I am not at all certain whether I actually wrote to you or if I just conversed with you in my thoughts on one of my strolls, as I have done time and again for many years . . ."

He jumped when the bathroom door suddenly flew open and the baroness showed herself in a pale purple bathrobe, let out a scream, and slammed the door shut again. A connecting door? Had she listened in on what we had been talking about? He was just barely able to notice that the baroness had hardly any hair on her head and her face looked much older.

Shortly before that, he had almost told Krakauer, "Why bother with prose if you can have poetry?" and had had the baroness and her niece in mind when he had thought it. How stupid, he thought, you can't say that.

He thanked Krakauer for the examination and said goodbye. And added that he wanted to drive down to Zell am See himself soon to buy a present for his wife.

"I finally got my hands on *Die Presse* for you." The head waiter handed him the newspaper, tucked in the wooden clamps in such a way that H. could grab the stick, and added, "I must apologize, but the *Journal* is nowhere to be found."

A gentleman wearing a top hat in the rear area of the coffeehouse irritated him. His groomed mustache immediately made him think of Poldy. Few wore such hats anymore, even in Vienna. Another gentleman sitting at his table was dressed in a winter coat, and each time he guided the coffee cup to his mouth he put his other hand on a newspaper as if afraid he might lose it. The penal sentence for Herr Hitler, who was currently held at Landsberg Prison, had been reduced, he read.

What was it that flashed through his mind? In the old Café Central, when he had been talking to Peter Altenberg about some support, about possible financial backers, somebody had flitted by like a phantom, had returned, had placed a series of pictures on their table, no larger than playing cards, colored views of the city of Vienna. After a while, he had come back over from the other side, had collected the artworks again, as if it had been a mistake. Altenberg, who had been mingling in the shadiest taverns, had said that this artist Hitler would one day be talked about far and wide. At night, when somebody bought him a pint or a bowl of soup, Altenberg said, he would give the wildest political speeches, and many of the wretched masses would hang on his every word. So, now he's writing a book, H. read in *Die Presse*.

A railroad workers' strike in Styria. He turned the page. The newly appointed commissioner Dr. Hornik was said to have liquidated forty thousand officials of the former imperial military bureaucracy, another sixty thousand state officials were to be relieved of their duties following the approval of the staff council ... Seven million kilograms worth of files sold as wastepaper ... The new currency was to be introduced that year still: Ten thousand inflationary kronen to one schilling—which in Vienna they were already calling the Alpine dollar. He started reading a Frenchman's essay about the tenth anniversary of the outbreak of the war, ignoring the disgruntlement that the memory of the summer of nineteen hundred and fourteen immediately aroused in him. Even more disgruntled was he by the associations the author's name pro-voked: André Germain. "What is the path we have trodden toward peace or toward war since the 1st of August 1914? Of what does our progress or regress or at least our standstill consist?" Germain mentioned the League of Nations: "I have no wish to join the optimists who believe that the mystical (and so convoluted) incantation of the League of Nations will bring about the golden age . . . " Carl would not like this, he thought. Then about the reestablishment of the Bayreuth Festival: "A professor from Tübingen wants to name Richard Wagner the leader of the German species, against Judaism and Americanization . . . "

He had been sitting in the church for a while. With his parents, he remembered, August had usually not been the month to visit Fusch; for the most part they had spent August on Lake Wolfgang. His father, of course, had returned to Vienna earlier each time; it had not been possible for him to stay away from his banking business for six or eight weeks.

Those years . . . the emperor's birthday, the festivities in Bad Ischl . . . (One year they had been in Fusch that day after all: the time when his mother had fallen ill before their departure and they had had to extend their stay.) Those jaunty weeks on Lake Wolfgang! Tennis, sailing, swim-ming . . . What long distances he had traveled on foot with his friends . . . He remembered an afternoon when he had hiked to the river crossing in Strobl with Michi Bebenburg, with Edgar, and his sister Lorle, whence they let themselves be taken to Sankt Wolfgang. He had wanted to show Edgar the Michael Pacher altarpiece, and had wanted to see it himself; one could never get enough of it. And then the long walk back to Strobl around half the lake in the evening. Today or tomorrow, he would telephone Gerty in Aussee and tell her the day of his departure.

He hoped for another encounter with Doctor Krakauer. The concierge had told him that Baroness Trattnig would stay at least another week in Bad Fusch.

He stood on the stone platform in front of the church. Strange—it was raining lightly, gossamer threads. The sun had been shining not long before, it had been warm, he had thrown on his frock coat. As he descended to the well, he noticed that giant leaves of coltsfoot were growing around it; everything was damp, the path sodden as if it had been raining for days. He had never noticed the sheer size of the leaves. The well's water pressure also seemed to have increased since this morning. He had forgotten to ask the concierge why the hotel had been hung with flags. The emperor—a silly reflex. Even if the emperor were still alive, it was another eleven days until his birthday.

On the water's surface in the well's trough, as he leaned over it, he saw, refracted by the waves and circles, his face. And he thought, I look young today, as though drawn or painted by Fernand Khnopff.

How long had it been? An entire lifetime, it seemed to him. Lisl Nicolics had sent him a postcard to Fusch, with a woman's portrait by Khnopff on the front. That was the time he had forgotten to buy two tickets for his parents at the resort building, for a famous artist's concert in the evening. It had been the emperor's birthday, August 18. All the hotels had been decked with flags, and he had to fetch blankets and seat cushions from the concierge. Roman Podschinsky had been the name of the pianist. It had been a fun summer, in spite of Mama's illness.

He had been with the musician Kreil and the painter Guggenmoser the evening before, they'd had a jolly good time, one of them had bought a bottle of wine . . . But later, at eleven, in his room, he had been too tired to sit down with his books and notes.

He lingered at the well, delighting in the painterly shapes that the pipe's thin trickle created on the surface of the water in the trough—along with glinting effects, although the sun had already set behind the Tauern mountain ridge. His parents had extended their stay for two weeks; on the scheduled day of their departure his mother had suffered a terrible fit of nerves. Nothing had come of the excursion, of the plan to take the recently completed rack railway up to Hohensalzburg Fortress.

It had been the year Frau von Wertheimstein died before she could leave for her summer retreat.

The weeks in Fusch saw the creation of terze rime that arose from her memory.

> How can it be that these latter days
> Are gone, forever gone, elapsed completely?
> . . .

To know that life now flows quietly
From her sleepy limbs
To the trees and grass . . .

The death of his dear friend and patroness had pervaded him for the duration of the vacation, and he had contemplated a few times whether—quite incomprehensibly—his grief might have been the reason he had been able to work so well in those weeks. Exhilarating ideas, they had veritably washed over him. He had often written for ten hours a day, the terze rime, drafts for novellas, for other poems. The only thing he had expected before embarking on the strenuous journey had been merely dreadful exhaustion. The prior months of cramming, the state examination at the faculty of law . . . The thought of working seems so terribly foreign to me, he had felt on his first day in Fusch.

Actually, he had thought, I usually have barely three, four good months a year, in which I have no trouble writing—at home, in the Brühl, on the Semmering—and this year, the examination has cost me two months . . . Although there had been some poetic thoughts, ideas, or fragments of things he had read that had haunted his mind while he read the law books. He could not, for instance, get the thought *that everything slips and flows away* out of his head.

"Where on earth did *that* come from?" his father had asked on a stroll when H. recited the line.

The English art critic Walter Pater had cited a sentence from Plato's *Cratylus* in his Renaissance study that was originally from Heraclitus: All things give way; nothing remains. In the letter he had written earlier to Hermann Bahr, he had mentioned making an important discovery: Pater, his *Imaginary Portraits*, that wonderful essay on Giorgione.

The sheet on which he had noted down Heraclitus's thought was where the lines of the first terze rime had been created, whose point of departure had been a memory: the visits to Döbling, on the property of the Wertheimsteins, in that beautiful garden, the table underneath the linden tree, where he had sat alone for many a half-day reading and writing but sometimes also studying for the exam. Then again, in the big house, the old woman in her armchair, the kiss on the hand, her strong odor, mixed with the scent of lilac...

Also his friendship with Marie, her niece, an amorous liaison almost, had been on his mind repeatedly. This unspeakably loveable and beautiful young woman, so strong and strong-willed in some respects and so unstable on the other hand—he had had to end it, had slowly put some distance between her and himself. What had been painful about this was that she herself had known long before him that she was too weak, too feeble for an amorous relationship, much less a bond for life. Every tremor, whether menacing or elicited by happiness, had to be avoided with her, her sister Franziska had told him once, when they had happened upon each other in front of the Minoritenkirche.

The old woman, he had thought at the time, has lived out her days in a higher and nobler existence than we regular people. She has given and received more precious things and dreamt richer and better dreams than perhaps all of us. How deeply this creature's traces will be imprinted on my future, he had thought. In everything that might become of me.

Another line from that time was haunting his mind: *I still feel her breath*... Or better yet: *Still I feel her breath*... But I did use that to start the series of terze rime, he recalled.

He would never forget the dream in which Michi appeared to him, Michi Nicolics, Edgar's sweetheart. H. had not been in love with Michi, but when official matters had caused Edgar to arrive in Strobl one week later than scheduled, Michi and he had grown closer. In his dream she had appeared to him as a little girl and at the same time as a completely erotic creature—very different from reality. When he had noted down the dream in the morning, the line evolved into a terza rima:

> Sometimes women who were never loved
> As little girls appear to us in dreams
> Unutterably moving sights to see...

As far as Marie von Gomperz was concerned: First the military service, he had thought, the voluntary year in Moravia, which he had to report for in the fall. That would create some distance. Who knows how I will feel thereafter. Professionally, he had no path before him. I am, he had said to himself, not rich enough, and will never be, to live a decent life without a profession. A scholarly career? Secondary school teacher? Go into civil service? Fantasy eludes me, he thought,

I cannot imagine anything at the moment. He remembered Grillparzer, the image showing him at a desk in his court chamber office.

How he had been looking forward to that evening. After dinner he would say goodbye to his parents, change clothes, work on his poems in his room. The evening before had been incredibly amusing, but in actuality it was time wasted. He could take his pleasure in Strobl, go sailing next week on Lake Wolfgang, play tennis, go for strolls with his friends. Strobl had never been a place to work for him. He had often asked himself what Strobl was missing and what Fusch gave him . . .

How he had enjoyed sitting a spell by the open window before going to bed back then, when the temperatures were pleasant, like now. He had sometimes heard a piano playing from the resort building, other times dogs barking, a kind of dialogue. One time he had walked all the way to the old farm, from where one could look down the steep incline onto the village. With fascination he had watched as the farmer's wife, surrounded by children, used a kind of wooden shovel with a long shaft to pull out the freshly baked loaves of bread from the oven.

And he also still remembered that evening very well: It was midnight, he was very tired. First he had been in his room, after dinner, had then gone downstairs to the smoking lounge, had sat for half an hour at the table where Gustav Schwarzkopf had been playing tarot with Carl Weis and a Hungarian music publisher. I am too dumb to play cards, he had told them, too much is shooting through my mind, I cannot focus on the cards. He was glad that the two had come to Fusch that year, he'd had nobody to talk to besides them, only Papa, on their strolls. A few days earlier, Schwarzkopf had handed him the manuscript for a comedy and had asked him to critique it. The Schwarzkopf family had also been staying at Hotel Flatscher since time immemorial. For many years, H.'s parents had been cultivating a close relationship with the family that owned the place. In the dining room he would sit with his parents; during the day, he would sit by himself, except when he joined the two men on a hike. He was glad not to encounter them during meals. Sometimes, when he went on solitary walks, he picked a bunch of flowers for Mama on his way back. How glad he had been when she had started feeling better.

Some days, his room had been dreadfully cold, he remembered; he had put on gloves to write. In the unheated reading room, he had fenced with a young Englishman to warm up, they had simply pushed the table and a few chairs aside. After a heavy thunderstorm, summer had returned overnight, with the ground shaking as if from a light earth tremor. The sodden paths dried quickly in the sun. Braving the horrible weather, the doctor had come up in his one-horse carriage, had examined his mother. Two days later, all three of them had gone on a hike again.

That evening he had gone for a walk to the church after dinner, joined by the painter Guggenmoser and the shy musician Kreil. A clear, starry night. He had resolved to walk to the high plateau on his own one day, around this time of night, with a flashlight to look up at the starry sky. Kreil had played a melancholy tune on the pale blue harmonium between the two storm lamps in the church. Afterward, the three of them had improvised scenes from old Italian novellas by Bandello, had strolled to the town's limits with the storm lamps. There had been no one left on the streets. They imagined that they were gallant gentlemen walking behind their torchbearers to the house of a woman they adored.

On the terrace, old Leo was unfurling some sunshades. H. chose a wind-sheltered table along the building wall. An interview in the *Interessante Blatt* with Franz Werfel about his Verdi novel. Once again he thought of Carl: On one of his last days in Lenzerheide he had wanted to write Gerty a letter about him, this remarkable man, about whom he was anxious at times, about the darkness of his nature, which, while it did not show very often, sometimes . . . His aversion to, nay, his hatred of Basel, his resentment for the historian's profession . . . He had wanted to tell Gerty that he suspected something calamitous in the characters of Carl's parents: the all-too intellectual quality of his father and the muted, earthy nature of his mother, who seemed never to have been happy in her entire life.

Doctor Krakauer was running late. They had agreed that they, the baroness's constitution permitting, would stroll to the completely dilapidated hunting lodge of the Cardinal

Prince zu Schwarzenberg, to whom Bad Fusch of the previous century had owed a lot. The baroness wasn't feeling well, Krakauer had told him in the morning when they met in the foyer, she would stay in her room all day. He would be available in the afternoon.

As Krakauer had told him that he had read *The Letter of Lord Chandos* with immense pleasure, he had opened the book to the first page himself, and had recalled the difficult years before and after his marriage. I entered life, he had once thought, years later, and my poetic abilities exited through the other door.

He hadn't been back to Fusch in those years, not until the year he had finally been able to finish the play *Venice Preserved* and in between had been working on drafts for his adaptation of ancient dramas and plays by Calderón.

Almost four weeks he had been away from home now, and what had he done? Nothing but notes for *Timon*, a few corrections, but the *Tower* was almost finished . . . Am I, he wondered, afraid to lose my way in my revisions once I get back to Aussee, to sense inadequacies, to draft new variants?

From a certain section of his head, as if it were an archive overseen by the likes of Franz Grillparzer, the novel, the Andreas character, occasionally called out to him, as if the character wanted to know what was going to happen in its life. The two seductive Venetian girls, about whom not even he, the author, knew—were they really two or was it just one making a fool of him? The boy, he thought, cannot possibly know that he is dealing with a split personality. And suddenly a thought about whether it hadn't been thoroughly wrong to connect the Romana story with that psychological case study the Princess of Thurn and Taxis had brought to his attention many years ago. Why not simply construct the Venice part as a wonderful time of apprenticeship for Andreas, with the Maltese knight as a kind of mentor; a love story also for the wholly inexperienced young man, or two love stories, in which Andreas would eventually decide to take Romana.

Eighteenth-century Venice, what a world for the son of a Viennese burgher family.

Romana, the girl the heavenly powers seemed to have granted him. The title of a painting by Titian came to his mind: *Heavenly Love and Earthly Love*. Romana and the Venetian girl. The Maltese knight, who was a mystery even to him, the author...The friends to whom he had read the fleshed-out pages had been enamored, had urged him to finish the book...Whenever he—as he had done some years ago in Altaussee—had devoted himself to the manuscript, the massive collection of notes and variations, of excerpts, references to further reading left him battered. After all, these notes constantly generated further notes, the pile of paper seemed to him increasingly like an endless mountain range, like the Höllengebirge or the Totes Gebirge near Aussee, which he had wanted to climb in his youth but never did. Seeing that fifteen-year-old girl during an evening procession in Aussee in the nineties had made such an unforgettable impression that when he began writing the novel in South Tyrol, at that Eppan Castle, he gave the Carinthian farmer's daughter the name Romana. It was there, at Eppan Castle, that he also began writing *The Letters of the Man Who Returned*, he remembered. He asked himself whether his parents would have let him travel to Venice and spend a few months there on his own at age nineteen. The Venice of the nineteenth century was no longer the Venice of around seventeen hundred and eighty, however, but probably still adventuresome, colorful, dangerous enough for an inexperienced young man.

At least, he thought, his parents had had no objections when he had traveled alone on his bicycle—some routes by train, however—from Salzburg, starting in Fusch, to South Tyrol, and from there via Verona to Varese; even though Mama had confessed to him afterward that her nerves had always been on edge during those weeks.

In Lenzerheide, on one of their hikes, he had told Carl about the *Andreas* novel and had promised to let him read (or read to him) what he had worked out so far when they would meet in late autumn in Aussee. Maybe Carl had an idea of how to continue and complete the story. Balzac's painter Frenhofer came to his mind again, who painted over his work so often, even his friends couldn't recognize anything on the canvas; this thought always made him feel queasy.

Was it Brecht who had pointed out Ludwig Tieck's novel fragment *Franz Sternbald's Journeys* to him and how in his later years Tieck was said to have kept mentioning to friends that he had wanted to finish the novel, which never happened?

Why had he gotten so wound up in the *Timon* play? Because he did not want to put yet another unfinished play in the cabinet with the other fragments? To Carl he had admitted—he remembered exactly where they had been standing: in front of the gigantic four-poster bed in the Palazzo Salis in Soglio—that he felt like a person who had failed in the second half of his life. "Please, let's leave that topic be!" he had exclaimed as Carl began to protest, and had thought: You have no idea what it really looks like inside me.

He had wanted to quiz Carl about Robert Walser before realizing that that was off-limits at the moment. In his room at the Park Hotel, he had recalled that they had met one time in Berlin. Walser had seemed to him like the son of a gentleman farmer, stuck in a dark suit for a wedding.

After a strenuous yet mentally refreshing long walk on the ridgeway toward Weixelbachhöhe, he entered his room impatiently, put the cane in the corner by the door, placed his hat on the unmade bed, immediately sat down at the desk to make some notes. He had known this for a long time: Things would occur to him if he didn't take his notebook, and if he put it in his pocket, its sheets would often remain empty. Of course, the idea of having the hetaera Bacchis appear in the second scene and involving her in a dialogue with Timon had already occurred to him days ago. But now he suddenly had the feeling that he was able to put the dialogue to paper, at least to sketch it without reading Plato's *Symposium* again beforehand. He suppressed the urge to go drink some tea downstairs; he could always take a break later and ...

Somebody had knocked at his door. Maybe it was Kreszenz, who finally wanted to make his bed. She should also fetch me a pot of tea, then, he thought and opened the door. A blond young woman wearing a white hairband, puffy white blouse, a large bow on her chest. Elisabeth?

"Elisabeth Trattnig, my apologies for barging ... "

"Has something happened?"

She seemed distressed. She said she was embarrassed. What does she want from me, he thought, what has happened? She reminded him of a young Alma Mahler.

"I apologize," he said, "as you can see, I cannot even offer you a chair at this moment."

Could she talk to him briefly? It was important, she said, it was about Doctor Krakauer. Perhaps it was better to talk in the reading room, nobody was there at present, she had checked. He took the manuscript bundle from the chair, pushed it to the middle of the room, pointed to it, sat down on the bed. She seemed attractive with her wavy hair, the full upper arms, he thought she resembled Christiane Vulpius as Goethe had drawn her. She walked over to the chair, leaned on the rounded backrest with her hand.

"Dear Fräulein von Trattnig, tell me, what happened?"

He got back up and tried to remember where he had put his spectacle case. He must have lost it. He noticed a hint of mustache growth on her upper lip; that, too, reminded him of Alma.

"The baroness," she said. "I don't know if you've heard that she went missing for a day; she just went off into the woods . . . I don't want to . . . She was found by two local boys, fairly disoriented. The doctor is beside himself with reproach. She blames him for having neglected her recently. That is why I have taken the liberty of addressing you."

"I have barely seen the doctor in the last few days," he said, a bit too loudly, and thought about where he put his spectacle case. "Just once, if I remember correctly, we had a longer conversation . . . Maybe twice."

Now he saw the case on the windowsill.

"I beg you," she exclaimed, "you don't know the gravity of the situation. The baroness's health has deteriorated . . . Severe depression, bordering on psychosis, and then her taking offense, her shocking resentment toward the doctor."

One keeps hearing about such nervous infirmities, he thought. He had read, however, that, unlike twenty, thirty years ago, these afflictions now barely occurred anymore since the war . . .

"She has been refusing to see the doctor the whole morning. There is a danger that she might . . . She insinuated something to the effect yesterday. She had wanted— and I know nothing specific about the matter—to set up a medical practice for him in the first district of Vienna in a few years' time, if they should part ways one day . . . This was the agreement between the two of them, but, as far as I know, only a verbal one. I'm sure it's not easy for the doctor, the baroness depends upon him in a certain manner. Please, you must excuse me, I feel terrible about having bothered you, it is just that I worry so much ... May I ask when you will return to Vienna? The baroness is completely unfit to travel at the moment."

The gall, he thought, they want me out of the way—thinking, my first impression wasn't so wrong, after all. That's all I needed, what do I have to do with all this? At the same time, he realized how much he liked her cultivated Viennese accent, her mellifluous voice. He wished she could have turned to him in a different matter, or that he could have heard her sing at the resort. But if she had approached him about his connections with theaters or opera directors or some such thing, as he had initially thought she might, he would have also found that annoying at this moment.

It suddenly occurred to him that he had, in fact, always imagined someone like her as the Egyptian Helena. She had hiked up her skirt before she had sat down, now he was looking, as if compelled by an obsession, at her naked knee and the naked part of her thighs.

Her rolling eyes, as if she were mutely singing a section from *Lucia di Lammermoor*. He also remembered what he had recently written to Poldy about the photograph of his sweetheart or future bride—who knows? And he wondered whether Elisabeth was a cold person. And he remembered that one could actually turn the constellation of Krakauer–baroness–Elisabeth into a one-act play. Arthur Schnitzler, he thought, would have shown no reluctance to do it. He looked at the uneven old floorboards that creaked with every step. The small table stood on a colorful rag rug, and there was another one in front of the bed.

"I'm sorry, but I'm afraid I must get ready now," he said, and stood up. "Someone is expecting me. I wish the baroness a speedy recovery. I'm sure she is in the best of hands with the doctor, isn't she? I hope she finds calm soon. Please extend my regards to the doctor."

"I beg your pardon. How foolish of me."

Her crystal-clear voice, he would have liked to ask her whether she had ever sung or rehearsed the Queen of the Night.

*Dear friend, stayed in Switzerland for a while but have now once again been residing here in Fusch for almost a week, where I have been so many times, as you know, mostly with my parents, so many times that I, when I want to reminisce, get confused about the stays.*

*I hope soon to breathe a kind of air that does not paralyze the free movement of my thought. The wrong air makes a dullard of me. As soon as my daily work, which occurs as if in a fever, is over, I am so drained that I am almost incapable of even holding a pen. The barometer simply must climb for once—how could I tolerate leaving this work unfinished? It seems to me that I am less and less able to tolerate such desolate highlands with firs.*

He stopped writing, scrunched up the letter sheet. Time for dinner. If he remembered correctly, he had written two or three letters and cards to Richard Beer-Hofmann in the last months, while the addressee had responded not even once. He went over to the wardrobe and looked for a clean shirt. Ask Vroni or Kreszenz to wash and iron two of them. And he thought, dispense with everything and walk away. Like the plumber at home last winter. When he had seen the condition of the water pipes in the building, he had simply left. The apprentice had packed up the tools and said to Gerty about his master: "Well, now he's ditched everything." What was that character called in the Raimund play?

He remembered that he was now as old as his father had been the year he had suddenly fallen ill here in Fusch. Is that possible? he thought, I'm as old now as my father was then, how did that happen? Rappelkopf was the name of the landowner in *The King of the Alps*. Where did the paper go on which he had noted down the departure time of the postal bus to Zell am See? The table was full of books, mail, notes, newspapers. And stones he had picked up on his walks, which he would return to nature. He should have long known by now that the most beautiful patterns on the wet stones would fade as soon as they dried. He bit into the slice of milk bread, which he had brought upstairs with him from breakfast.

Tell Gerty that this milk bread tastes just as good as ours at home, from the Grünbaum bakery. Why even ride down to Zell am See? So he wouldn't bring anything from his trip this time. He dreaded packing his luggage without his wife's help.

He remembered Max Reinhardt, the two giant dogs, which now were probably romping around the park of his palace in Leopoldskron. But he didn't even know whether Reinhardt was spending this summer in Salzburg. He never got in touch, he thought, it always has to be me who writes or calls or inquires. Kitchen scents poured in through the window; it now dawned on him that the wing in which he was accommodated was located above the hotel kitchen. He picked up his son's letter again, Raimund, the son who was better able to deal with life, as people said, the one most like him. He felt the same way, and yet he often sensed that Franz was even closer to his heart.

How he looked forward to seeing both of them soon.

After all, he had had Christiane staying with him for the last months; she wanted to go back to Paris in autumn. Her friendship or love for Thankmar von Münchhausen was something he could not figure out. The young man did not seem to suffer terribly from the current long separation. Luckily, the child had already put her first heartbreak behind her and could now be friends with Erwin Lang. The times that follow, he thought, don't hurt as horribly.

He should have reached the treeless, high plateau with the level meadow trail by now; he should have long been sitting on the Embachalm terrace—which he had been looking forward to since this morning—over milk and buttered bread and a view of the mountain panorama. Yet he seemed to be advancing ever deeper into a forest, in which he no longer knew the way.

Which forest might this be? After all, the wooded hill spreading out at a gentle incline behind the church was not big, at least not in his memory. Had the forest expanded so much in thirty years? The trunks stood ever tighter side by side, it became darker and darker, he had broken a sweat, it would be better to turn around. Who, he thought, wouldn't think of the beginning of the *Divine Comedy* now: "I went astray from the straight road and woke to find myself alone in a dark wood . . ."

I, too, need a Virgil, someone to guide me, he thought, and since I did not bring my Fusch hiking guide, I won't even be able to check how and why I got lost once I'm back in my room again. In any case, it would have been better to hike from the town along the Fürstenweg to the fork toward the ridgeway and then make a left turn toward the cabin. In the past, his heart had always soared on this path, beyond the constrictions of the hamlet's buildings and the surrounding steep slopes.

He turned his head. There was no longer a recognizable path, he had to turn around. All the fir and spruce trunks were branchless up to a very tall height. Views of the sky there were few. What am I doing here?

He longed to be in the Stallburggasse, in his small city apartment in Vienna. To climb down the stairs there now and drink a black coffee at the Café Bräunerhof . . . But to skip up the stairs to the third floor like my father used to, it dawned on him, I couldn't do that anymore. How often had Gerty and he changed clothes up there, before going to the theater or a concert, slept there on the folding bed afterward, had breakfast in the coffeehouse the next morning, done some shopping, and then at their leisure taken the tramway to Rodaun. The many small antique shops on that street, before the war, the little Biedermeier table Gerty would have loved to have—and then suddenly it had been sold.

How he had, he remembered, sung the praises of Bad Fusch, this *magical place*, to Carl on his last day in Lenzerheide . . .

Halfway up a tree trunk an animal yipped, a squirrel, as he saw now, it waved its tail excitedly, looking down at him. Many years ago, somebody had told him that all the slopes in Bad Fusch had been forested because of the frequent avalanches. From afar he heard a dog barking. So, I still haven't left this world yet, he thought.

It had been Director Flatscher himself, he remembered, and Flatscher had also told him about a logger whose thigh had been sliced open by a boar's tusks; the man had slowly bled to death in the woods. What member of the imperial family was it about whom somebody many years ago had told a similar story, which, however, was said to have ended a lot less grimly, because one of the hunters had been a doctor?

To imagine the path our history, he thought, might have taken, had the emperor died in his younger years or in midlife. It would have had to have happened at least forty years ago, when the crown prince had still been master of his own faculties. The emperor's birthday at least would be commemorated in Altaussee. It couldn't be any other way. (To imagine that the birthday of some politician might mean something to anyone!) At about this time of the year, some people in Aussee would have been already able to collect ripe fruit from the ground in the garden. In the fall, when the apples lay underneath the trees each morning, the landlady, usually at the crack of day, while they were all still asleep, came with a basket and carried away the nicest ones.

He suddenly felt deeply exhausted, longed for a bench to rest, but had seen only a single one on the way here, at the beginning of his hike; it had been so completely overgrown by young spruces that only a squirrel or a fox could have used it as a seat. He had to persevere, could not even estimate how long. Upon entering the forest, along the trail that started with a gradual incline, he had thought about a phrase Novalis had written that most sounds nature produced were spiritless, yet the rustle and whistle of the wind seemed melodic and meaningful to musical souls. Perhaps my memory deceives me, he said to himself, and that's not at all how the sentence goes.

The young hotel employee who had knocked brought a letter to his bed. H. tried to sit up a bit.

"I will give you something later," he said.

*Esteemed Herr Hofmannsthal,*
*My baroness is afraid the weather will once again take a*

turn for the worse, despite forecasts to the contrary, and suddenly urges that we depart. She is very serious about it; hence only a few brief lines, should we fail to meet again. I would have loved to talk to you especially about your Man Who Returned, *which I have now been able to read in its entirety! Very impressive, the final letter, about the colors. After having read the first of the letters, I was almost afraid of bumping into you again.*

*I may not be a citizen of Germany, but it seemed to me upon reading this philosophical narrative that some of the things you disliked about the people in Germany—for your man who returned, am I right, is in fact you—also apply to me . . . Twice I knocked on your door yesterday, to no avail.*

*Yet you don't wish to depart until the day after tomorrow, the concierge has told me. We are going home, to the baroness's estate in Fratres in the Waldviertel. I hope to be able to get in touch with you in late autumn, when you will have returned to Rodaun.*

*Sebastian Krakauer*

Literature, painting, and music mean little or nothing, he had often thought, when one falls ill. Everything fades away, one only wants to regain that original state of well-being. Entirely elemental desires at the moment: to drink coffee in the hotel's sunroom, to read a few new newspapers, to go for strolls, to ride to Salzburg on the omnibus . . .

Diagonally opposite, in the Hotel Berghof, on the other side of the street, on his level, on the third floor, a lady, wearing a kind of turban on her head, had opened the window and looked out, looked over, saw him standing at the window, and promptly closed her window again.

He still hoped that Doctor Krakauer would knock on his door, would have a quarter of an hour for him before departing with his baroness. Today to Salzburg, and tomorrow to Lower Austria, Krakauer had said yesterday. One conversation . . . Even if little time remained, at least they could exchange addresses, and perhaps continue their conversation about *The Man Who Returned* in Vienna or Rodaun, he had thought.

In any case, he would also be departing shortly; he had already told the concierge so yesterday. When he leaned out the window to his left, steadying himself with his right arm on the windowsill, he saw three automobiles in the parking lot. He believed he saw the baroness's Steyr, with the roof up; so they had not departed yet, he realized, were probably still busy packing.

If I had to explain to somebody, he thought, why a conversation with Krakauer seems so important to me . . .

He saw himself sitting in front of the house in Altaussee, in a few days' time, telling Gerty about his new idea of writing a longer piece based on *The Letters of the Man Who Returned*, a novella perhaps, and to include the postwar years. Krakauer had given him the idea, when he had told H. a few days ago about how he had returned to Austria from the United States in nineteen hundred and nineteen. Once again, he shook his head about himself: My problem, which seems insurmountable, is that I always want to create something out of everything right away.

On the page with the advertisements, he could not, for a long while, take his eyes off the two automobiles; he especially liked the new Opel.

"A car for everyman. 4 hp, complete, three thousand nine hundred *goldmarks*, pick up from Rüsselsheim factory."

He and his wife had long been wanting to get a car of their own, like many of their friends, but who was supposed to drive it? How much might it cost to hire a chauffeur on occasion? The car's shape seemed to him aesthetically perfect, simply beautiful. But who knows when one might be able to buy the car in Vienna.

On the front page of the *Frankfurter Zeitung*—last week's, a guest must have left it—a feature by Joseph Roth, who, as one could read in the lead, was currently staying on the island of Rügen. He heard the bells of Fusch church jingling, the Angelus. Roth reported of a dance event, fishermen and fisherwomen in old traditional costumes. An old fisherman later complained at the tavern table that the young fishermen did not place any value on heritage and would rather dance jazz and shimmy.

Recently he had read an extremely riveting, full-page, tightly spaced travel report from Iraq by a journalist named Leopold Weiss. Starting from Aleppo, the adventurous four-day desert journey to Baghdad. Had I read this at home, he thought, I would have had the atlas on the table to look for all the sites. With great concern, he read about the enormous hatred of the Iraqi people for the British Empire, to which Iraq had been granted after the collapse of the Ottoman Empire, and about the Iraqis' struggle for freedom. At the end, the travelers got into an insurrection in the great bazaar. Carl's travel report came to his mind, his *Travels in Asia Minor*, which H. would publish in the next issue of the *Deutsche Beiträge*. He reread the last paragraph: "...a rattling sound, as if someone were spilling dry peas on the floor..."

He realized that reading this had upset him. And he decided to go upstairs now, to lie down again for a bit, and later, after dinner, to go for a short stroll, if it wasn't too dark then. Since the newspaper didn't seem to belong to anybody, he folded the double-page with the feature and put it in his pocket. Then, in Aussee, he would tell his family about this article. His wife had said time and again that when he talked about travel accounts he had read, one could imagine the foreign lands better than if someone who had been there did the reporting.

What time of day is it? Afternoon, probably. The way the light flooded through the open window was something he had observed only in Aussee. Had someone knocked? Where was the door?

"One moment!"

He sat up, looked down at himself, the rumpled nightshirt. Dizziness, again. No matter, it could only be Kreszenz or Vroni, anyway. He remembered a conversation many years ago in Paris—was it with Paul Zifferer? How they had talked about the seventeenth and eighteenth centuries, that the higher nobility did not know embarrassment, not only in front of the servants, but that even friends and acquaintances were received from one's bed ... He tried to get up. Dizziness, again, immediately.

"Yes, please!"

Is that ... ? Doctor Krakauer.

"I apologize, my sincerest apologies! The concierge told me—very discreetly, by the way, he knows that I'm a doctor—that you are not feeling well. How are you? Has the resort's physician examined you?"

"I took on a little too much," he replied, "steep trails ... I know it, and I did it anyway. *Hardened arteries*, dear Herr Doktor, my internist in Vienna already told me two years ago ...

"I lost my way, yesterday afternoon, like your baroness the other day, isn't that right? Sometimes it seems to me as if the mountains and hills around Fusch have shifted, apparently new forests have sprung up ... In any case, nature is in flux. Ever since they got the avalanches under control, the landslides are now ... My apologies. Would you like to move the books from the chair ... ? I imagined you were long ..."

Krakauer hesitated, looked around the room.

"Just put the things on the floor and come sit by my bed for a while, if you have the time. These ... excuse me, Thonet chairs are known to be quite uncomfortable to sit on. I've asked for a second chair, one I can actually sit on. This one may only be good as a storage place ... My tongue feels as if it were paralyzed, sometimes, since yesterday ... Yes, the doctor. Doctor Seywald ... He suspects that I have sustained a slight stroke ... At any rate, I am happy to see you."

Thank God, he thought, the chamber pot has been emptied, so Kreszenz was here, after all, and he felt embarrassed because of the crumpled pants hanging over the board at the foot of the bedstead. Two years ago, he said and ran both his hands through his thinning hair, he had already had a small episode like that. He simply wanted to stay in bed today, tomorrow he would hopefully be able to get up again. He pointed at the chair once more.

"Yes, I only have a moment, everything is already stowed away. But I simply could not allow myself to get in and drive off without saying goodbye to you first. The concierge only knew that you had called for the doctor."

The package on the table—had Kreszenz left today's mail for him? He pondered trying once more to slowly sit up. On the night table the pills, handkerchiefs. On the table a plate with two apples and a knife and the *Timon* folder. In the morning he had read the three successful pages a few times, the Bacchis dialogue. Developing something from that should, by all means, be possible ...

"Strange, isn't it, Herr Doktor, this morning, when I felt dizzy as soon as I tried to get out of bed, I immediately thought of my father. Here in Bad Fusch, many years ago—I was about twenty. A few days after our arrival, my father— we had spent at least three weeks each year in July up here since my childhood, mainly because the altitude, the climate, and the medicinal springs were good for my mother ... So, my father fell ill, spent two days in bed, and I was quite scared: Mother had often been ailing, but not my father. At the time he must have been around the age I am now, about fifty. Every once in a while, I went up to the door to my parents' room, pressed my ear against the door, listening to see if I could hear anything ... My father got up on the third day. He had refused offers to have the doctor from Zell am See come here, had insisted on going on a little tour."

"You, too, will recover, trust me. There are very good remedies these days to expand the blood vessels. As I've said before, you must promise me to get examined at the General Hospital as soon as you are back in Vienna. Can I have someone fetch you anything else?"

H. sat up, wedged his two pillows to adjust them.

"Unfortunately, I'm already far behind schedule; they are expecting me, but I don't care what the baroness says now. If everything goes well, we will be in Fratres tomorrow, and I will feel much freer. And I will think about the direction my life should take. You look so pale, and I cannot do anything for you at the moment, unfortunately ... You should be very cautious with your smoking."

But I don't even smoke, he thought and waved Krakauer goodbye. He tried to sit up again in bed, and stated with satisfaction that his dizziness was now almost imperceptible. And wondered whether it was true that the good doctors emanated healing waves.

"I would need *another go* . . . you may remember? My son brought this word from . . . I would need many years to finish some things. So much of what I started seemed promising and ultimately wasn't viable."

"But you have created so much."

"I don't know which author from the past century said that he had lived mistakenly for fifty years, further years in uncertainty and fear, and only very late had begun to understand what one could do and what one should leave undone. That brings me to my *Death of Titian*, which I recently reread, after so many years, in the new edition of collected works. The great Titian, at age ninety-nine, says in my play that all his old works are amateurish tinkering, that it is only now that he has attained certainty. Until the hour of his death he paints his *Pan*, whom he portrays as a veiled figure. It is only at his end that he stops being an amateur. At the time, at the age of eighteen, I surrounded Titian with young students and young admirers, as if I had sensed what I myself, late in life, would let nobody . . . But forgive me, please, don't let me keep you."

"I am so sorry, how I would love to keep listening to you right now!"

All the windows in the glass wall of the palace of flies were open. He remembered how so many years before, in the similar but much smaller terrace-like sunroom of their hotel, his mother had complained over and over about all the flies; where on earth did they—and sometimes the wasps—all come from . . . Incidentally, the Park Hotel in Lenzerheide had also been unable to ward off the flies; a few times, Carl had had an almost hysterical reaction to the flies on their table.

He still regretted that Carl, who had been late anyway, hadn't shown up for breakfast that day in Lenzerheide a few minutes later, instead of at exactly the moment he had wanted to inconspicuously rip that page from the newspaper. What he would give now for this *feuilleton* page with Robert Walser's prose poem! I am still not master of my own faculties, he thought. Walser had struck him as an impertinent fellow, back then—how many years ago?—at that reception in the publisher Samuel Fischer's residence in Berlin. Walser had suddenly approached him, clearly a bit drunk, and exclaimed, "Can't you ever forget that you are famous?" Before that, as H. had been conversing with the publisher's wife, she, as Walser passed by them in mountaineering boots, an empty glass in hand, had been telling him what Walser had said about Rilke: that his books belonged on the nightstands of old spinsters. This had at least amused him, but then he had hoped that Walser wouldn't say the same about his own books and had walked to the adjacent room to look for his publisher. He had remembered something he wanted to tell Fischer regarding the planned edition of his prose works. He thought, years ago I put Walser on the list of contributors for my journal *Morgen*, but Borchardt, the coeditor, objected: He had read the new novel *The Tanners*, Rudolf had written, which served only to cause him a few hours of discomfort.

The cucumber salad he'd had for lunch crept up his esophagus.

By now, all the tables and chairs were occupied, Sacher torte and apple strudel on every table—no wonder, then, that the room was teeming with insects. Midsummer had finally arrived in Fusch, he thought, now that his departure was imminent. He sat on the edge of the glazed terrace; this was the best seat still available. On his right-hand side, he could look out the windows to the Weixel streambed, which now flowed so calmly one could not even hear it at all.

A remark by Eckermann in his *Conversations with Goethe*, which H. had remembered the night he had not been able to sleep, preoccupied his mind once again. It had become clear to him that right now he simply could not transport himself onto the busy square in third-century Athens: Goethe, Eckermann said, had told the story of how he had written the play *Götz von Berlichingen* as a young man of twenty-two, and hadn't personally experienced any of the relationships and events. So he had to use *anticipation* to put himself into the position of plausibly depicting this world and bringing it to life.

In the nineties was when he had read this passage from Eckermann's conversations with Goethe to his father at home in Vienna—a few days after his father had exclaimed, in the middle of reading the first act of *Ascanio and Gioconda*, "Where on earth did all that come from; you are starting to scare me." Goethe, he had replied to his father's words, hadn't lived in the sixteenth century, either.

At the time, he thought, I read Bandello's novellas—as well as some other things; and not to forget, there were times when I went to the Kunsthistorisches Museum almost daily to stand in front of paintings by Titian and Giorgione—nonetheless, there must have also been some kind of anticipation at play. The character of Gioconda was intertwined with Marie von Gomperz, which he had not been able to tell his father . . . Indeed, he was often under the impression that Marie was from a different century. But already *The Death of Titian*, conceived before *Ascanio and Gioconda*, before his acquaintance with Marie, was set in Renaissance times. His father had not understood how he could think and feel his way into the existence of such an ancient painter . . .

The buzzing and humming of all the flies was indeed irksome. He put on his eyeglasses and tried to inconspicuously look over at the gentleman who had entered moments ago and seemed to be staring at him. With the glasses on he could be even less certain whether he knew the man. The man was blocking the path of the waiter, who had wanted to hurry past him with a fully loaded tray, and the waiter said something to him. Now the man started moving, walking toward him. H. felt his heart tighten. Was it Rudolf Borchardt? What a weird notion, he immediately thought, I imagined that same thing a few days ago . . . Am I finally going senile?

On the other hand, the slender, dark-skinned face, the mustache, the stiff gait of an officer? I wouldn't mind, he thought, reconciling with Rudolf. Visiting Borchardt, before the war, in his beautiful villa in the countryside, near Lucca, built on a hillside, surrounded by olive trees, pecking chicken, and turkeys in front of the house, a spring with wonderful water behind the house . . . That had been in nineteen hundred and twelve, the year of *Ariadne*. Exciting, stimulating conversations throughout the whole day, late into the night . . . How they had both revealed themselves to each other as they had taken their leave: This encounter had renewed their friendship . . . Forgotten, what the publisher Willy Wiegand had once told him late at night: that Borchardt had not only nice things to say about him; in a late-night circle in Berlin he had once opined, "Hofmannsthal? Oh yes, a restless literary man of the world, always bent on making an impression; never at a loss as to how to attain such an impression . . ." Enough. Everything, everything was counterbalanced by that long letter in which Rudolf had written him some things about his *Ariadne* . . . Who in Germany—in Austria even—H. thought almost with a kind of envy, but a good kind of envy, *envidia sana*, as the Spanish say—who would be capable of writing in such a way about a poetic construction?

As the man approached, his face now seemed somewhat rounder; now he was looking past H., striding past him in hobnailed shoes, hat in hand.

That time in Fusch when his father had been in bed sick for two days . . . It was the year of his secondary school graduation, he remembered. He could not get the thought out of his head that he, too, had now reached that age—fifty—and

131

that his father seemed to have been in much better physical shape than he was now... The temporary heart problems must have been the consequence of excessive work.

He remembered how boisterously Papa had almost skipped down the stairs to the church back then, on the way back from a mountain hike, such that Mama had anxiously called after him. What was it, he tried to remember, that I was working on at the time? Stopped his *Titian*, forced to interrupt the work to cram for his school diploma, and then no longer able to find his way back into these intimate dialogues... Started writing *Ascanio and Gioconda* that summer.

Marie von Gomperz... That summer, during a visit to Aussee, he had made the acquaintance of her aunt, Frau von Wertheimstein, which he had been wishing to do for a long time. How had Hermann Bahr put it once, on a stroll up the Kapuzinerberg in Salzburg: In life you achieve everything you wish for, but too late, you do it when it no longer gives you joy... That might have been the case for Bahr, but I, he thought, couldn't say that the things I dreamt of in my younger years would one day... Some things did. And what else could I hope for? And was I not spoiled at a very young age, was my lyrical work not praised throughout the German-speaking world? Have I not made a name for myself without realizing how it came about? And isn't the important thing now to tie the beginning up with the ending... But how would I get there? Hadn't the path to becoming a playwright been a blind alley? Didn't even my friends praise my essayistic work more than my theater works, excepting the

*Rosenkavalier*? Even the Germanist Josef Nadler, he remembered, only lauded the prose works; he had even written to Nadler once inquiring whether he wouldn't give consideration to his lyrical stage pieces.

He remembered that this time Krakauer had not responded to the desire expressed for *another go*. What did this mean? Was his illness really incurable?

What on earth is the point of all this? he thought. Why can't I be at home in Rodaun, on my sofa in the study or in the bedroom, and let Gerty take care of me? It seemed to him that he was so infinitely far from home that it was highly questionable whether he would ever return there.

*Dear Carl, I send my belated apologies to you for my sudden departure, but who if not a friend would understand it all. My conversations with you continue, even without your presence and for want of letter paper . . . Also* Timon *is occupying my thoughts again. I must devise a farewell speech for the envoy, an apostrophe to beauty before he sacrifices himself to death . . . But perhaps he shall be saved by the foreign slave at the last minute . . . The erstwhile Weilguni Hotel now has the name Grand Hotel. People on the terrace are conversing about the Dawes Plan or the border traffic restrictions with Germany . . .*

He remembered that the day before, while he had been drinking coffee in the sunroom, it had occurred to him that this stage here would readily lend itself to a performance of the *Great World Theater*; all the necessary characters were there—well, except a king and a beggar . . . and the two angels. What guides us out of the labyrinth, he thought, is language. Everything, he had realized in his younger years, was dependent on us constantly rethinking the true meaning of our words. Perhaps it would be a boon, in inauspicious times like these, when language is degraded to mere convention, to be silent for a while, much like I have tried to demonstrate in my Lord Chandos letter. All my friends, and I myself, for a long time did not understand that I anticipated my own future with this letter. But I, unlike Lord Chandos, have failed, have been unwilling to bear the consequences, the abandonment of all literary activity... Of course, I first sought a way out of my misery, turned my attention to the art of dance, to pantomime, wrote libretti for the dancer Grete Wiesenthal. Again, these were just words... But I, with my family in the background, could not start *dancing*...

He had finally found the passage in *The Death of Titian* that had been on his mind. The old artist, on his sickbed, wishes to see some of his old pictures one more time:

> *He says he must see them...*
> *The old, the pathetic, the pale ones,*
> *To compare them with the new ones he paints...*
> *The hardest things have now become clear,*
> *An outrageous understanding gaining ground*
> *That until now he has been a dilettante...*

I would, he thought, very much like to know now how I thought of such sentences back then, at the age of eighteen.

*To compare them with the new ones he paints . . .*

For the third time, he heard the honking of the automobile. He sat up in bed. That honking, again. He opened the window, which was when a long piece of putty peeled off and fell into the courtyard. Two automobiles were downstairs, one behind the other, facing the exit. The first car was leaving the premises, rolling slowly, with heavily smoldering exhaust, across the bridge, down toward the town of Fusch, to Bruck, into the world . . . A person in the back was holding up a white kerchief, waving. Only now did he notice in the driver's seat of the second car, whose motor was not turned on yet, a person covered in leather attire, looking up at him. Now he was even waving at him. But who was again pressing that horn? Was it Krakauer, finally ready to leave, who wanted to shout one more thing at him? If only I were ready, too, he wished.

On the other hand, he was looking forward to the stroll, the barometric condition could not be better at the moment. He leaned out a bit, waved back. And took off his glasses. But he could not see who it was.

Now he heard a woman's unpleasantly loud voice coming from a window on his level:

"Yes, yes, for the love of God, I'm coming!"

He quickly retreated. How stupid of me, he thought. It was nothing.

WALTER KAPPACHER, born in 1938, is an Austrian novelist who has won many German language literary awards including the prestigious Georg Büchner Prize. He has written short stories and novels as well as radio and screenplays, and lives near Salzburg.

GEORG BAUER is a Vienna-based translator and editor. He is the 2021 recipient of the Austrian Cultural Forum New York Translation Prize for *Palace of Flies*.

### DISTANT FATHERS
### BY MARINA JARRE

This singular autobiography unfurls from the author's native Latvia during the 1920s and '30s and expands southward to the Italian countryside. In distinctive writing as poetic as it is precise, Marina Jarre depicts an exceptionally multinational and complicated family. This memoir probes questions of time, language, womanhood, belonging and estrangement, while asking what homeland can be for those who have none, or many more than one.

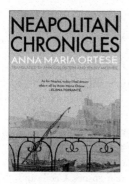

### NEAPOLITAN CHRONICLES
### BY ANNA MARIA ORTESE

A classic of European literature, this superb collection of fiction and reportage is set in Italy's most vibrant and turbulent metropolis—Naples—in the immediate aftermath of World War Two. These writings helped inspire Elena Ferrante's best-selling novels and she has expressed deep admiration for Ortese.

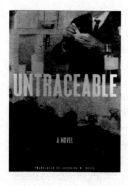

### UNTRACEABLE
### BY SERGEI LEBEDEV

An extraordinary Russian novel about poisons of all kinds: physical, moral and political. Professor Kalitin is a ruthless, narcissistic chemist who has developed an untraceable lethal poison called Neophyte while working in a secret city on an island in the Russian far east. When the Soviet Union collapses, he defects to the West in a riveting tale through which Lebedev probes the ethical responsibilities of scientists providing modern tyrants with ever newer instruments of retribution and control.

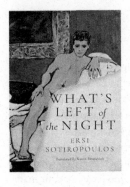

### *What's Left of the Night*
### by Ersi Sotiropoulos

Constantine Cavafy arrives in Paris in 1897 on a trip that will deeply shape his future and push him toward his poetic inclination. With this lyrical novel, tinged with an hallucinatory eroticism that unfolds over three unforgettable days, celebrated Greek author Ersi Sotiropoulos depicts Cavafy in the midst of a journey of self-discovery across a continent on the brink of massive change. A stunning portrait of a budding author—before he became C.P. Cavafy, one of the 20th century's greatest poets—that illuminates the complex relationship of art, life, and the erotic desires that trigger creativity.

### *The 6:41 to Paris*
### by Jean-Philippe Blondel

Cécile, a stylish 47-year-old, has spent the weekend visiting her parents outside Paris. By Monday morning, she's exhausted. These trips back home are stressful and she settles into a train compartment with an empty seat beside her. But it's soon occupied by a man she recognizes as Philippe Leduc, with whom she had a passionate affair that ended in her brutal humiliation 30 years ago. In the fraught hour and a half that ensues, Cécile and Philippe hurtle towards the French capital in a psychological thriller about the pain and promise of past romance.

### *The Bishop's Bedroom*
### by Piero Chiara

World War Two has just come to an end and there's a yearning for renewal. A man in his thirties is sailing on Lake Maggiore in northern Italy, hoping to put off the inevitable return to work. Dropping anchor in a small, fashionable port, he meets the enigmatic owner of a nearby villa. The two form an uneasy bond, recognizing in each other a shared taste for idling and erotic adventure. A sultry, stylish psychological thriller executed with supreme literary finesse.

### THE EYE
### BY PHILIPPE COSTAMAGNA

It's a rare and secret profession, comprising a few dozen people around the world equipped with a mysterious mixture of knowledge and innate sensibility. Summoned to Swiss bank vaults, Fifth Avenue apartments, and Tokyo storerooms, they are entrusted by collectors, dealers, and museums to decide if a coveted picture is real or fake and to determine if it was painted by Leonardo da Vinci or Raphael. *The Eye* lifts the veil on the rarified world of connoisseurs devoted to the authentication and discovery of Old Master artworks.

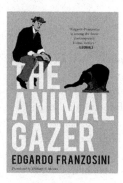

### THE ANIMAL GAZER
### BY EDGARDO FRANZOSINI

A hypnotic novel inspired by the strange and fascinating life of sculptor Rembrandt Bugatti, brother of the fabled automaker. Bugatti obsessively observes and sculpts the baboons, giraffes, and panthers in European zoos, finding empathy with their plight and identifying with their life in captivity. Rembrandt Bugatti's work, now being rediscovered, is displayed in major art museums around the world and routinely fetches large sums at auction. Edgardo Franzosini recreates the young artist's life with intense lyricism, passion, and sensitivity.

### ALLMEN AND THE DRAGONFLIES
### BY MARTIN SUTER

Johann Friedrich von Allmen has exhausted his family fortune by living in Old World grandeur despite present-day financial constraints. Forced to downscale, Allmen inhabits the garden house of his former Zurich estate, attended by his Guatemalan butler, Carlos. This is the first of a series of humorous, fast-paced detective novels devoted to a memorable gentleman thief. A thrilling art heist escapade infused with European high culture and luxury that doesn't shy away from the darker side of human nature.

### THE MADELEINE PROJECT
### BY CLARA BEAUDOUX

A young woman moves into a Paris apartment and discovers a storage room filled with the belongings of the previous owner, a certain Madeleine who died in her late nineties, and whose treasured possessions nobody seems to want. In an audacious act of journalism driven by personal curiosity and humane tenderness, Clara Beaudoux embarks on *The Madeleine Project*, documenting what she finds on Twitter with text and photographs, introducing the world to an unsung 20th century figure.

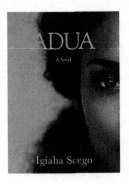

### ADUA
### BY IGIABA SCEGO

Adua, an immigrant from Somalia to Italy, has lived in Rome for nearly forty years. She came seeking freedom from a strict father and an oppressive regime, but her dreams of film stardom ended in shame. Now that the civil war in Somalia is over, her homeland calls her. She must decide whether to return and reclaim her inheritance, but also how to take charge of her own story and build a future.

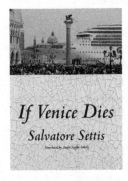

### IF VENICE DIES
### BY SALVATORE SETTIS

Internationally renowned art historian Salvatore Settis ignites a new debate about the Pearl of the Adriatic and cultural patrimony at large. In this fiery blend of history and cultural analysis, Settis argues that "hit-and-run" visitors are turning Venice and other landmark urban settings into shopping malls and theme parks. This is a passionate plea to secure the soul of Venice, written with consummate authority, wide-ranging erudition and élan.

### THE MADONNA OF NOTRE DAME
### BY ALEXIS RAGOUGNEAU

Fifty thousand people jam into Notre Dame Cathedral to celebrate the Feast of the Assumption. The next morning, a beautiful young woman clothed in white kneels at prayer in a cathedral side chapel. But when someone accidentally bumps against her, her body collapses. She has been murdered. This thrilling novel illuminates shadowy corners of the world's most famous cathedral, shedding light on good and evil with suspense, compassion and wry humor.

### THE LAST WEYNFELDT
### BY MARTIN SUTER

Adrian Weynfeldt is an art expert in an international auction house, a bachelor in his mid-fifties living in a grand Zurich apartment filled with costly paintings and antiques. Always correct and well-mannered, he's given up on love until one night—entirely out of character for him—Weynfeldt decides to take home a ravishing but unaccountable young woman and gets embroiled in an art forgery scheme that threatens his buttoned up existence. This refined page-turner moves behind elegant bourgeois facades into darker recesses of the heart.

### MOVING THE PALACE
### BY CHARIF MAJDALANI

A young Lebanese adventurer explores the wilds of Africa, encountering an eccentric English colonel in Sudan and enlisting in his service. In this lush chronicle of far-flung adventure, the military recruit crosses paths with a compatriot who has dismantled a sumptuous palace and is transporting it across the continent on a camel caravan. This is a captivating modern-day Odyssey in the tradition of Bruce Chatwin and Paul Theroux.

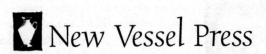

New Vessel Press

*To purchase these titles and for more information
please visit newvesselpress.com.*